Rachel

MW00942009

The Story

By
R.C. Fletcher

Cover by Hannah-Marie Kilpatrick

Prologue: Seven Years Ago . . .

Rachel Andric squealed, partly in fear, partly in amusement, as her older brother Ewan chased her through the garden of the Andric family mansion. For the first time in a week, the sun was shining brightly in the brilliant blue sky, pushing away the heavy dark clouds of rain that had lurked over the island for seven days. Rachel and Ewan's parents, Miriam and Philip Andric, stood on the wraparound porch, leaning on the two white columns next to the stairs. They laughed at the antics of their children, who were overjoyed to finally get out of the stuffy house.

Ewan, who was about two heads taller than Rachel, used his much longer legs to catch up to his little sister and tackle her from behind. They rolled to the ground, giggling uncontrollably. "I have caught you, fair maiden!" he pronounced between laughs. Although usually he acted like fourteen-going-on-fifty, the temptation to play with his little sister like they used to was occasionally too much for the boy. Besides, with just the four of them on the lonely island, there wasn't exactly a whole lot else to do. "Now I shall bring you to my draconian lair and *eat* you!"

Rachel squealed again, struggling as Ewan wrapped his arms around her waist and picked her up. She seemed to be having fun but was scared out of her wits at the same time. Before Ewan could follow through with his threat, their parents came over. Philip gently extricated Rachel from her brother's arms and placed her on his shoulder. "I shall save you, damsel in distress," he said, teasingly poking her nose with his free hand.

Rachel made a face, her usual no-nonsense personality reasserting itself. "I would have saved myself," she said, wrinkling her nose. "I'm not a defenseless princess."

"Oh, really?" Ewan challenged her. "Then how come you were at my mercy?"

"That's enough," interrupted their mother, Mimi, as Philip called her. Both of the kids immediately fell silent, and Philip grinned at his wife. She had a commanding presence that brooked no argument from the children. He, on the other hand, was definitely the fun parent. "Ewan, your father and I have important business to take care of. Keep yourselves out of trouble, both of you. We'll be back soon," Mimi went on.

"You're leaving?" Ewan said, clearly disappointed. "I thought we could have some, you know, *family* time."

Philip ruffled his son's raven hair—the only blonde Andric was Rachel. "There'll be plenty of time for that when we come back," he promised. "It's just a routine mission. We won't be gone for very long."

"Where are you going?" Rachel asked. She was a bit of a bookworm with more interest in Philip and Mimi's tales about The Story than going into The Story Book itself.

"Sherwood Forest," Philip told her. "Someone's in danger of dying when they shouldn't be. It's a relatively simple task for the two of us, right, Mimi?" He gave his wife a cheeky wink.

She returned the wink with a trademark frown, tossing her black curls over her shoulder irritably. "Don't get cocky," she warned him in her thick British accent, her light blue eyes flashing in an annoyed way. "You don't want to pass any bad habits onto the children, would you?"

"Right." Philip ran a hand through his close-cut hair with his free hand, trying to hide his embarrassment. Rachel squirmed from her high position, and he set her gently on the ground. Her Andric eyes—clear blue eyes—blinked up at him, looking concerned. "Wind's picking up," he went on, trying to ignore the strange looks his children were sending him. "Keep

3

an eye out for a storm. Ready, Mimi?" Unlike his wife, Philip and their children were all in possession of American accents.

His wife gave a grim nod and kissed both her children on the forehead. Philip followed suit, earning a smile from Rachel. However, Ewan's brow was furrowed as he watched his parents. Philip and Mimi left their children there, winding their way over the stone path through their well-tended garden and up the steps of their porch. Standing on the porch, they both instinctively turned back to Rachel and Ewan. Rachel waved with another smile, but Ewan was still watching them with that strange look on his face. Philip tried not to shudder at the intensity of the stare; it was far too serious for a boy of Ewan's age.

Mimi opened the front door and led Philip through the house he'd lived in his entire life. Although there weren't many windows, casting a rather dark gloom over the many skinny hallways, electric lights powered by magic illuminated the darkness. Family pictures of both Philip's past and their current family lined the walls from the ground floor, all the way up the staircase to the second floor. The tan carpet that was on the floor of the entire house felt plush beneath Philip's feet, the only reason they kept it. Mimi, however, despised it.

Finally, after climbing up the straight maple stairs with the smooth railing, they turned to the second room on the right at the top of the stairs. It was always kept locked and Philip produced the key from his pocket. "Ready?" he said.

"Of course I'm ready. We're wasting time," Mimi replied impatiently, but the impatience failed to reach her face.

They went through the door together and Philip took a moment to breathe in the room that contained what they were protecting—The Story Book. As Guardians, it was their

4

life's work to defend it from all harm. The small, square room was unfurnished aside from the pedestal with a glass covering right in the middle of the room, housing an ancient book. The two stood just inside the door for a moment. When Philip spoke, his voice was quiet. "Look at this place. It's a place people dream about. The book—all the Stories ever told in the world, right at our fingertips."

"Fairy tales, myths, legends." Mimi sighed. It was a conversation they always had whenever they went into The Story together. "And old friends as well. Yet all of them can be deadly, Phil. Can you imagine what would happen if one of the times we go in that book, it could be our last? I mean, I don't want it to be, but ... what if it is? What if we leave the children alone?" *Like our own families,* was the unspoken thought between them.

Philip put his arm around her comfortingly. "We made a promise not to leave the kids, remember?" he reminded her. "This won't be the last time we see them. There never will be a last time, okay?" He kissed her forehead, all signs of his jocular nature gone. "Now, come on. There's a boy who need saving, and I know you wouldn't leave him there to die."

She nodded silently, and together, they lifted the glass covering from The Story Book and laid it down on the floor. The ancient book flipped open to the page they wanted and they both exchanged long looks. "To Sherwood Forest, then," Mimi said.

Philip laced his fingers through Mimi's. "To protect The Story," he agreed. They laid their hands on the pages and a brief flash of light illuminated the dark room. When it faded, there was no sign of Philip or Mimi.

Ewan came in the room silently, taking in the emptiness. He glanced behind him once before placing his own

5

hand on the book. Again, the light came and went, pulling him into The Story itself.

Chapter 1: The Intruder

Wind and rain lashed at the island mercilessly, the only light to brighten the gloom being the occasional lightning bolt. One such bolt illuminated the white-clad form of the island's only inhabitant, Rachel Andric, as she walked through the stony path in the badly-neglected garden. The wind tossed about her rain-soaked blonde curls and tugged at her nightgown, heavy from the weight of the rain.

The girl herself paid little heed to either the storm or its discomforts. She walked slowly in her slippers, hugging her arms to her body. The humidity of the island was choking, mingling sweat on her brow with the rain. Due to the storm, the mansion's magically-induced power had been knocked out and it was no cooler in there than outside. "What good is magic if it can't even keep the power going?" she mumbled to herself, her voice light and airy as would be expected from a girl of her short and thin stature.

Her wanderings took her to one of the cliffs leading down to the beach on the end of the island. Rachel gazed across the black ocean, using one pale hand to keep her curls out of her face. She didn't know how many times she had gone to the cliff in the seven years since her parents' deaths. It had provided solace, particularly following Ewan …

If she closed her eyes, she could still see Ewan coming up to her, handing her a practice sword their father had crafted them from wood. *"Come on, Rach!"* he'd say. *"King Arthur wouldn't cancel a duel of honor over a little rain! Fight me!"* Then he'd lash out with the sword, always holding back with his blows.

Rachel cupped her hand over her mouth, choking back a sob that came to her throat. "Five years," she whispered, "and I still miss you, Ewan. Why doesn't it get any easier? Why did you have to go?"

The only answer was a rumble of thunder, directly above her head. It was followed immediately by a bolt of jagged purple lightning, illuminating the unused dock built over the beach. Something attracted Rachel's gaze over there, and she peered through the slashing, pouring rain. "Where's another lightning bolt when you need it?" she muttered, trying to decide what had caught her attention.

As if in response to her words, another rumble, followed by a blinding flash of lightning. Still, peering hard, she saw something that definitely shouldn't have been moored to the dock—a motorboat. Her eyes widened and she picked her way down the cliff, accidentally sliding the last few feet down and cutting open the back of her right leg. Still, she made it to the bottom and went over the dock.

Sure enough, the motorboat had been recently tied to the dock, tossed cruelly around by the black waves. She stared at it for several seconds, her brain refusing to comprehend what it meant. A boat, on her uninhabited island … without warning, she spun around and ran for the path leading back up the cliff. As she went, she kicked off her slippers—they would have made running almost impossible.

Barefoot, in her pajamas, with her tousled hair in matted curls around her shoulders, she sprinted for the house. She had no thought about what she planned to do with whoever had come to the island. Maybe they were lost and had been stranded on the ocean. But the odds of that were slim. The island was tiny, little more than an indistinct speck on a map. It would be nearly impossible to have come from the coast of America and actually managed to find it.

As she sprinted through the mud of the garden, she could see that the front door was ajar—and she knew she had closed it when she'd left. Fear started building up in her throat as she ran. Mud splattered her legs and caked her bare feet, but she just kept running.

Rachel pushed the door out of her way as she went inside. Once she'd closed the door behind her, the storm outside was a distant rumble. The stairs were an indistinct blur in the darkness, and she was forced to slow her pace, gripping the railing and feel each step out with her toes before moving up. The entire time, she was straining her ears, trying to hear whoever was in the house—but they were silent. Finally, after what felt like ages, she reached the top of the stairs and stopped dead in her tracks.

A big, burly man stood in front of a door at the top of the stairs. *The* door. Bile rose in her throat, and when she stepped on the landing, it creaked beneath her. He turned to face her, his face shadowed in the darkness. "Well," he said in a deep, gravelly voice. "If it isn't little Rachel Andric. I had expected more opposition than just you. Where's your brother, girl? Have your precious Guardians really left an inexperienced female to do a man's job?"

His casual use of the group Rachel belonged to alerted her to the fact that she wasn't dealing with a normal intruder. She approached slowly, still keeping several feet between them when she stopped. Her tongue felt like lead in her mouth as she forced herself to speak. "Who are you?" she asked. "Why have you come? There's nothing here for you."

"You know what I want," the man told her. "And I'm going to get it. You know you can't stop me."

When she spoke, her voice was far calmer than she actually felt. "The Story Book is my family's most valuable possession. I would give my life to protect it. It is my destiny to protect it."

9

"You, little more than a girl?" The man laughed hoarsely. "I am superior to you in every way, Rachel Andric. I have spent years planning this, far longer than you've been alive. Today is my day of triumph."

"Why wait until now?" Rachel said. "If you've been planning it for so long, why wait?"

"My reasons are my own. You know why I need you. It'll be better for you if you do as I say."

Rachel shook her head, backing away until half her foot was hanging over the top step. He approached her slowly, a malevolent expression on his face. "Don't even bother running, girl. You can't beat me, and where would you go?"

In answer to that, Rachel spun on her heel and ran down the stairs. She could hear him, only seconds behind her, and fear forced her feet to move. Once she'd reached the bottom of the stairs, she ran for the door, throwing it open and sprinting out into the rain. With her breath coming in ragged gasps, her heart beating in her head, and the rumbling of thunder, she could no longer hear her pursuer behind her. Somehow, though, she knew he was there.

Lightning flashed, and her hair obscured her vision. Soggy curls covered her face and her clothes stuck to her from the rain. Pebbles dug into her bare feet and mud caked the soles, splashing up onto her legs as she fled. Rain mixed with the salty tears of pure terror on her cheeks. If he were to catch her, if he were to *make* her do what he wanted her to do ... everything her family had done would be worthless.

To be honest, she had no idea what she'd do. Would it be better if she just hurled herself at the mercy of the waves? If the man got his hands on her, it would have been better to be dead.

Without warning, the man snatched Rachel's hair and yanked her back. She screamed in pain, punching out at him.

There was a brief moment of startling agony through one of her wrists and he grunted in pain. "Behave yourself," he snarled, pinning her arms to her sides. Her small stature was a detriment and left her helpless in the man's grasp. Nevertheless, she kicked and struggled, trying to escape as he dragged her back to the house.

Fight as she did, Rachel could not keep the man from manhandling her back into the house and up the stairs. She may as well have been hitting a brick wall, for all the good it was doing her. In the end, as he pulled her through the hallway, she just went limp. Seconds later, they were in the room with The Story Book once again. The man shoved Rachel down to the floor, sending her tumbling. "Take the glass from the book," he ordered.

She picked herself up, shaking her head. "No."

The man crossed his arms. "I think you misunderstand me, Andric. I know that only those in your bloodline can lift the glass. And I'm not asking. You will lift the glass, or I will force you to lift the glass. And I don't think you'd enjoy that."

Rachel kept her back to the back, pressing herself against the column it sat upon. "Do what you want to me," she said, trying to act far braver than she felt. "You'll never force me to do what you want. Leave me in peace and go back to whatever hole you crawled out of!"

Moving swiftly, the man snatched Rachel's forearms, pulling her close to him again before spinning her around. He squeezed her wrists, causing her to cry out in pain. Somehow, she wrenched her left arm free and turned to him, slamming her fist into his nose. The shock of the blow reverberated up her wrist, and blood poured onto her bruised knuckles. With a snarl of pain, the man tossed her aside, clutching his broken nose in one hand. He cursed her savagely, advancing on her, but she didn't just stand around and listen to what he was saying. She ran for the book, grabbing the glass covering and swinging around again.

Rachel hurled the covering at the man, but his reflexes beat her by a split second and it sailed harmlessly over his head. The glass shattered against the wall, sprinkling down to the floor in tiny pieces. Cursing her stupidity, Rachel grabbed The Story Book and held it in her arms.

The man blocked her path to the door, blood caking his upper lip. The look on his face was one of intense rage and hatred. "You will not be leaving here alive," he vowed.

Rachel shook her head, clutching the book to her chest. "You misunderstand me," she told him, purposely using the sarcastic words he'd said to her earlier. "I *am* leaving here alive." She flipped open the book, laying her hand on one of the pages.

"NO!" the man shouted, and lunged at her.

"Enter The Story!" she yelled over him. It was not necessary to speak the words, but stress forced the words she was thinking out of her lips.

The man struck her at full force, knocking her backwards. The back of Rachel's head barely hit the column The Story Book had sat on, and the book fell from fingers. Still, she somehow kept the tips of her fingers on the pages. The man's hand fell beside her own as he grabbed at the book...

A blinding flash of light was the last thing Rachel as the air was pulled from her lungs, and she lost consciousness.

Chapter 2: Into The Story

Robin Hood of the Merry Men crept through the trees, intent on his prey. Although he was a tall and muscular man, he moved with the quiet certainty of a deer. Crouched in the hedges, he slid forward slowly, a hand on his sword at his side, the forest around him silent as the grave itself. Robin hardly dared to breathe as he neared the large man on the path ...

"Robin!" The loud calling of his name seemed to boom throughout the entire forest. Robin flinched and stood erect, brushing leaves and twigs from his forest-colored clothes. The big man turned to face him, his face nearly concealed by his uncontrollable dark brown hair and beard. "What the devil were you doing, sneaking up on me like that?"

Robin scowled, dropping his hand from his sword. "How do you always know?" he asked in a defeated tone.

The man grinned, his teeth surprisingly white behind his tawny skin and dark beard. "The forest is too quiet. When I can't hear anything, I know you're there."

Robin sighed, clapping a hand on his friend's shoulder. "This is why we are the Merry Men," he said. "We all have our abilities, and yours is an uncanny sense of logic, John. Among other things," he added with a little grin.

Little John grew more serious. "Did you find the boy?"

Robin's light eyes slid to the ground. "No."

John gently laid a hand on Robin's shoulder. "Don't worry, old friend," he said soothingly. "He'll turn up sooner rather than later. Alan was checking Nottingham. If he's not in the dungeons there, then there's still hope."

"What if he's been killed in the forest?"

John shook his head. "I think there's little fear of that. He's a Merry Man, Robin, though he's a young one. Getting killed in the forest is simply an impossibility for us."

"Robin! Robin Hood!" The familiar, higher-pitched voice snapped through the forest like an unwelcome arrow. Robin sighed and turned as the strangely-tall, gangling figure of the Bard of Sherwood Forest came running up. The young man, in his mid-twenties, with reddish-brown hair, panted for breath, holding up his hand to hold off any questions.

In spite of himself, Robin leaned closer to the bard. "Alan," he said urgently, "have you found Will?"

To Robin's immense disappointment, Alan-a-Dale shook his head. "No, Robin. He's not in the dungeons at Nottingham, nor anywhere else in the city," he replied. "Least, not that I saw." Even out of breath as Alan was, his voice still came at twice the speed of a normal person's way of speaking.

Little John gave Alan a disapproving look. "You came all this way in such a hurry to report ... failure?" he asked.

Alan rolled his dark eyes. "I'm not just reporting failure," he said. "There's a man at the campsite. Says he wants to speak to Robin."

Both men turned to Robin, who frowned. "A man?" he answered. "What man?"

"I don't know," Alan admitted. "He wouldn't give his name. He just said—"

"That he wants to speak to me, yes, I'm aware," Robin grumbled. He looked up at the dark sky, sighing. "Another day without the boy. Where in the world could he be? Alright, men, let's head back to camp and meet this fellow."

.   .   .   .   .

14

For quite a while, Rachel drifted in and out of consciousness. She didn't know where she was, but the first thing she could vaguely remember was her face pressed against dirt, twigs digging into her cheeks. It hadn't taken her long to black out again from the dull, thudding pain in her head, and when she came to a second time, she felt odd. There was a strange, bouncing sensation, almost like footsteps, and she could feel someone's arms around her.

When she woke for the third time, she no longer felt the desire to slip into unconsciousness again. Although there was still an uncomfortable pounding sensation in her skull, Rachel could actually think again. She didn't feel the dirt beneath her anymore. It was something harder, more unpleasant. Yet it was cushioned by something softer.

Slowly, Rachel raised her head. She appeared to be in some sort of a cave, or a rocky outcropping. Rain fell outside, slapping against leaves in an oddly soothing sound. A fire crackled in the cave, giving off a cheerful light. With a grimace, she put her hand to the back of her head, feeling her damp hair and something sticky on the crown of her head. When she pulled her hand away, her fingers were red with blood. She stared at the blood, smelling its sickly-sweet scent, and her breath started to come faster. It wasn't much, just a small scratch from where she'd hit her head, but bile rose in her throat all the same.

"Ah. You're awake."

The voice distracted Rachel from her illness and she raised her eyes. Across the fire, leaning on the opposite side of the cave, was a tall, skinny figure. She couldn't make out his features; her eyes were yet to adjust to the darkness. "Who ...?" she asked, her voice thick. Her tongue felt like a sponge in her mouth.

15

"Are you well?" The more the stranger spoke, the more Rachel could make out about his voice. It possessed a thick British accent and had a distinctly young quality to it. "I found you in the forest, unconscious, with blood all on the back of your head. I fear you were robbed and left in the rain."

"Robbed ..." She had been robbed, in a matter of speaking. Robbed of the family honor, of the family treasure. With startling clarity, she recalled everything that had happened at her home. And now ... it couldn't be.

Overwhelmed, she couldn't stop the tears from escaping her eyes. She covered her face with trembling hands, but that only made it worse—she could smell the blood on her fingers. There was a strange scrabbling sound, and she nearly jumped out of her skin when she felt a gentle hand on her shoulder. "I'm sorry. I didn't intend to upset you."

Rachel raised her eyes, seeing her companion's face for the first time. He was younger than she was by probably three or four years, freckles splashed across his ghostly-pale face. A stark contrast to his white skin was his dark red hair, curled around his boyish face. Sorrowful dark eyes looked at her pityingly. "You—you didn't," she managed, though she scooted away a little. Nobody had touched her so gently since Ewan ...

The boy pulled his hand away. "My apologies. Would you care for a drink?"

Considering that there was a lump in her throat, she nodded in answer to his question. He crawled back to the other side of the cave and returned a moment later with a canteen of water. "Here. Have all you want. I can get more."

She gratefully accepted it and drank about half of it. Once her thirst had been quenched, she looked away shyly. It occurred to her that she hadn't spoken to another human being in five years, aside from her attacker, and she didn't think that could be qualified as a normal conversation. "Thank you," she said.

"You're welcome, milady," the boy said, smiling. His cheeks dimpled. "Will, at your service. Will Scarlet."

Rachel's head jerked up and she stared at him. "Will … *Scarlet?*" she echoed. She knew him—from the Robin Hood legend. Seeing him in person, all she could think was how young he looked. The pictures in her books hadn't showed him so young. For the first time, it sunk in that she was really in The Story.

The very Story that had claimed her parents' lives. She pulled away from him.

"I'm sorry, have I said something wrong?" Will asked, looking as if she'd stung him.

Rachel forced a smile, brushing a soggy curl out of her eye. "Nothing. I'm sorry. I just feel a little …" She let her voice trail off.

Will cocked his head. "Your accent is a bit odd. Where are you from?"

"I'm … not from around here," she said. "I'd rather not say and mark myself as an even bigger foreigner."

That made the boy cock his head and shrug. "Very well. But I'm afraid I don't know your name?"

She flinched, realizing how rude she must seem to him. "Rachel. Rachel Andric."

"I've never heard of such a name before," he commented. "Please, make yourself comfortable, Lady Andric. I mean you no harm here. I wouldn't feel right sending you off on your own while you're still injured."

She managed another small smile, realizing there was a heavy cloak over her shoulders. Taking a peek beneath the cloak, she found herself clad in a dark red gown, soaking wet and heavy. Apparently, the magic of the Guardians—which enabled a Guardian to change their clothes to match the environment of their Story—had occurred without her knowing. "Is this ...?" She motioned to the cloak.

Will made a dismissive gesture with his hand. "It's nothing," he told her. "I don't need it." He flashed a grin, sitting back on his haunches. "I can try and clean the blood off the back of your head, if you want. Just to make it a little less itchy. I've been hit over the head before, it's not fun."

The thought of the blood matting her blonde hair together made Rachel have to swallow down bile once more. However, she nodded. "Please."

The boy gave her another smile—he seemed to do that a lot—and pulled a pack closer to him. After producing a cloth from the leather pack, he took the leather jug of water and dipped the scrap into the water. With a gentle hand, he started tending to the blood on the back of Rachel's head. Although it tugged uncomfortably at her hair, his ministering hands weren't hurting her. "Where did you learn to do this?" she asked.

Will gave a small shrug. "A man named Friar Tuck."

It was beyond strange for Rachel to hear Will speaking of the Merry Men with such familiarity. The words were a reminder to her that she had to be careful. If she accidentally said something about The Story, Will would recall it and her problems would increase by a large amount.

A member of The Story, like Will, lived through their Story repeatedly. Cinderella always lost her slipper, King Arthur always died to Mordred, and Hercules was always killed by his wife—accidentally. However, if a Guardian were to tell someone about the fact that they lived in The Story, they would remember all their past lives and most likely attempt to change whatever their fate would be.

It was the Guardians' job to ensure that The Story remained the same. If the intruder were to enter The Story and change things ... Rachel shuddered. "Milady?" Will's ministering hands stopped. "Have I hurt you?"

"N-no. It's okay. Carry on."

"Very well." Will continued and tended to her head wound. About twenty minutes later, he was evidently satisfied with his work and moved aside, placing the bloodied cloth to the side. "Better?"

Rachel tentatively touched the back of her head and felt only a little blood there. "Better," she replied. "Thank you, Will."

He smiled again, showing his dimples once more. "I'm glad, milady," he said. "I really am. I'd give you something to eat, but ... I haven't got anything. I've been a little ... well ... lost in the forest for a few days."

Rachel stared at him. There was something rather ridiculous about a Merry Man getting lost in the forest, particularly if her educated guess was right and they were in Sherwood Forest. "You've been lost?"

The boy must have detected her incredulity, because he blushed furiously. "It's not so difficult," he protested. "It's a big forest, and I'm ... I'm not the best with directions."

Perhaps the members of The Story were more human than Rachel had given them credit for. Still, she had to struggle to keep a straight face when she heard that one of the Merry Men had gotten lost. "I think I'm going to go to sleep," she said.

Will nodded. "Good night, then."

She curled up in her cloak and fell asleep after only a few minutes.

.   .   .   .   .

Robin, John, and Alan reached the Merry Men's campsite and were greeted by the balding, muscular Friar Tuck. The man's forehead was crinkled in anxiety. "Robin, where the devil have you been?" the friar said, sounding most distressed. "This man has been lurking around for hours!"

Robin sent Alan an irritated look. "What?" the bard said defensively. "It's a big forest. It took me a while to find you."

Mumbling darkly about the usefulness—or lack thereof—of his men, Robin proceeded through the trees to the clearing. Normally, the men's campsite was a place of boisterous chatter and laughter as they sat around the five campfires ringing the clearing. That day, however, the mood was darkened both by Will's disappearance and the presence of the burly stranger in the middle of the clearing.

Contrary to the rest of the men, who kept their distance from the stranger, Robin marched up to him and raised his chin up. Although Robin was tall, the other man was just the slightest bit taller. "You wished to see me?" Robin said, keeping his voice neutral. There was little point in antagonizing the man—yet.

"Robin Hood, I assume?" was the man's smooth response. However, his voice was roughened by the gravel in his throat.

Robin shrugged. "You can assume all you want. Why are you here? How did you find us?"

"I know much that you wouldn't expect," the man answered slyly. "Please, sit."

"I'd rather stand," Robin retorted. "You will state your business or leave. I would not be disappointed if you did the latter."

The burly man laughed. "Don't be so hostile, Robin. I only wish to talk. This could concern your missing lad, after all."

Robin tensed. "What do you know of Will?"

The man smirked. "Sir Guy of Gisborne is currently leading an attack to catch him. Unfortunately for you, they might not take him alive."

Robin lunged forward, grabbing the man around the neck. "Who has done this?" he snarled. The only way Gisborne could have known about Will was if someone had told him.

The man carefully extricated his neck from Robin's grasp. "Now, now, my friend," he said. "It wasn't me. You'd never believe me if I told you."

"Tell me or I snap your neck here and now!" Robin shouted.

"Oh, very well. No need to be so dramatic." The man rolled his neck. "It's a little blonde brat. A girl, with curly hair and the clearest blue eyes you've ever seen."

"A girl?" Robin looked at him, incredulous. "You're telling me a girl betrayed Will and resulted in this mess?"

The man nodded. "She is more than a mere girl," he said.

"Oh, really?" Sarcasm dripped into Robin's voice.

A sly smile crept over the man's face. "What do you know about ... The Story?"

Chapter 3: Sir Guy of Gisborne

Rachel woke slowly, her head still aching dully, but not nearly as bad as before. She sat up, the cloak falling from around her shoulders. Will Scarlet was curled up in a ball in the corner, fast asleep, snoring softly. He looked less like a Story character and more like a normal person, sleeping like that.

21

The young outlaw left her in a strange quandary. She needed to find the intruder—if he was still in the Robin Hood Story—but the longer she stayed with Will, the more chance there was something would go wrong. If she said something incorrect, it could remind him of The Story and change things. As a Guardian, she couldn't afford to have that mistake happen.

But if she left Will, questions could be raised. She had foolishly told him her real name, and if he were to talk about her, the intruder might hear of her. If he was still in Sherwood Forest. If he wasn't, then she wouldn't have a problem.

That settled it. She needed to leave Will's company and determine if the intruder was still in this Story. Although she didn't know the way, she was confident that she could find someone not important to The Story to direct her there. Will was one of the main Merry Men. Should she cause something to happen to him that normally *wouldn't* ...

Rachel gathered the satchel Will had left next to her and laced his cloak over her shoulders. Under normal circumstances, she would have felt bad about the stealing, but desperate times called for desperate measures. He was a Merry Man. Surely he could find his way back to the others at some point.

She crawled her way over to the exit of the rocky outcropping and prepared to depart. However, distant sounds made her freeze in her tracks and listen, very carefully. Tensed, frozen, she heard what sounded like thudding footsteps—but much heavier. Instinctively, she knew what they were. *Hoofbeats.*

Movement behind Rachel nearly made her heart jump out of her throat until Will crawled up beside her. "Oh, blast it all," he muttered. His red hair was smashed against the side of his head, where he'd been sleeping. "How did *he* find me when I don't even know where I am?!"

"Who?" Rachel asked, surreptitiously sliding the satchel back behind her, to make it look like she hadn't been trying to leave.

Will hesitated just long enough to let her know he knew what she'd been up to. "It's Guy of Gisborne," he said reluctantly. "He's found me."

Rachel swallowed, hiding her discomfort. She decided it would be best to play the fool. "Why would Guy of Gisborne be looking for you?"

For the first time, Will sent her an exasperated look that was probably brought on by nerves. "I'm an outlaw!" he said in frustration. "I'm one of the Merry Men."

Rachel's eyebrows shot up. "Maybe it's not the best idea for you to go spouting that off to any stranger you find in the forest?" She couldn't resist the suggestion.

"It doesn't even matter," Will said with an irritated sigh. "I'm going to get caught no matter what. I can already tell he's got us surrounded. Blast it!"

"Okay, okay," Rachel said. His tension was starting to wear off on her. "Let's just stay calm. There has to be a way out of this ..."

Will looked grim. He dug through the satchel Rachel had been in the process of stealing from him and procured a rope. "You're not going to like this," he said.

She eyed him a little nervously. The boy himself looked rather ill. "What?" she said.

"I'm going to have to make you my prisoner." Seeing the expression of sheer disbelief on her face, he hastily added, "It's the only way! Otherwise, Gisborne will arrest you as well. Maybe we can *both* make it out of this."

"Will ..." Rachel really didn't like that idea. Too much could go wrong. Gisborne could kill him for holding her prisoner, or realize they were bluffing. However, she could see there was no other way out of it. Sighing, she turned around and pressed her wrists together. "Do it," she said. It was a bad idea—a *terrible* idea—but there was nothing for it.

Will bound her wrists together tightly. Too tightly. She made a noise of complaint and the outlaw swiftly apologized, but didn't loosen the ropes. "It has to look genuine," he explained. "Gisborne'll know if I tied them too loosely. I'm sorry." To complete the ruse, Will tied an old rag around her mouth, efficiently gagging her.

She honestly couldn't decide if he really wanted to hold her prisoner or not. Everything she'd read about the Merry Men indicated that they were the heroes of their Story. Then again, the stories she'd read about them also claimed they were expert foresters. And Will had gotten lost ...

He guided her to the back of the cave and had her sit down back there. She eyed him a little anxiously, and he flashed her a nervous smile. "I'm sorry," he whispered.

Since there was a gag around her mouth, she couldn't answer. Instead, she just shrugged. There wasn't a whole lot she could do.

In a matter of moments, men marched into the outcropping, blocking all exits. Will pressed his back against the wall, Rachel crouched on the floor at his feet. Her gaze was firmly locked on the man who stepped forward, apart from the rest of the men. Even without having read the Robin Hood Story and seeing the pictures of him in it, Rachel would have known he was Guy of Gisborne. The commanding presence that seemed to surround him made sure of that.

He was younger than Rachel had thought—probably only a little older than she was. The old cliché about a man being tall, dark, and handsome somehow managed to apply to him. His black armor accentuated his well-toned muscles, and his raven hair contrasted his pale skin. Dark brown eyes surveyed the scene grimly, narrowing in disgust when they fell on Will. The outlaw had drawn his sword and held it close to Rachel's neck. Guy of Gisborne's hand fell from his undrawn sword and he motioned for his men to stay put. "Scarlet," he growled. "Have the Merry Men really sunk so low?" His deep voice almost had a lilting effect to it from his British accent.

On the flip side, Will's higher-pitched voice had a distinct nervous edge to it. "I have no desire to meet the hangman's noose," he replied. His hand was trembling, pressed against the back of Rachel's neck, holding her up. Quietly, she prayed that he wouldn't slip with the sword. "So step aside, Gisborne, unless you want the lady to be separated from her head."

The threat pushed Gisborne into action. He drew his sword, steel sliding against the leather scabbard sharply. Gisborne leveled the sword at Will, still several paces away. "You harm her, and your death will be slow and painful," he warned him. "Only the worst of cowards would hold a lady hostage and harm her."

"I'm not a coward," Will said softly. His grip was loosening on the back of Rachel's neck. He was losing it; Gisborne's words had taken seed in his mind. Rachel squirmed, trying to escape from his grasp, hoping to avoid having Will and Gisborne get into a swordfight. At least if Will ended up as a prisoner, she would still have a shot at rescuing him.

For if Will died at Gisborne's hands now, he would undergo the fate that all members of The Story feared—Final Death. Their character in The Story would have to be replaced, and the one who had undergone Final Death was gone. Permanently. Final Death only came about when tampering led to a change of fate for a person and they perished in a different way then was written in their Story.

This definitely qualified as a different way for Will.

Gisborne's eyes fell on Rachel once again, and he must have read the scared expression in her eyes. He couldn't have known the reason, but most likely assumed that she was terrified of Will. "You will let her go," he snapped.

Will glanced down at Rachel. She was still struggling to escape her bonds, fighting the ropes and panic at the same time. She still met his gaze, trying to transfer her concerns over his safety to him. Why did he not understand? "I cannot," Will said, turning back to Gisborne. "She is my security."

"Coward!" Gisborne's voice cut like a whip, and Will flinched. "Craven! Draw your sword and fight me like a man!"

No, no. That was a terrible idea. Rachel would have shouted at him to stop, but with the blasted gag around her mouth, she couldn't say or do anything. The outlaw, possibly sensing her disapproval, shoved her to the side and pointed his own sword at Gisborne. Rachel squirmed, trying to pick herself up off the ground, only to be grabbed beneath the arms and pulled to "safety" by one of Gisborne's men.

The man was too entranced by the beginning of the fight between Will and Gisborne to actually go to the trouble of releasing Rachel. She could do nothing but watch as the two men lunged at each other, their swords clashing in midair with sparks flying. The two were pressed close together, nose-to-nose, hatred bright in the other's eyes.

Will jumped back. His face was a ghostly white while his cheeks flamed red with effort. Gisborne narrowed his eyes, barely winded. Then Will jumped forward, bringing his sword whistling in from the left. *Clang.* Gisborne's sword caught ·

26

Will's, pushing it aside. His fist followed up, slamming into Will's face and sending the boy staggering back. "You cannot defeat me," Gisborne said disdainfully.

Will touched his cheek, blood staining his fingertips. Rachel focused her attention on Gisborne instead of the red trickling down Will's face. "You underestimate me," the outlaw said, drawing a knife and holding it in the opposite hand of his sword.

Again, the two men jumped at each other. Steel clanged on steel as their swords struck once more. This time, Will swept at Gisborne's chest with his knife. He underestimated the strength of Gisborne's breastplate and the knife bounced off uselessly. Will recoiled a pace when he was met with unexpected resistance.

The momentary weakness was sniffed out by Gisborne like a bloodhound. He struck like a snake, swinging his blade in the general direction of Will's head. The outlaw seemed to panic as he ducked, the sword whistling wickedly above his hair and missing him by inches. At this point, Rachel's heart was in her throat as she watched in an agony of suspense. She really wished there was something she could do other than watch.

Even though the initial strike from Gisborne had missed and Will had survived, Rachel had been taught about momentum in a battle. Will's momentum was going against him, the surprise from Gisborne's quick attack starting to get into his head. As he caught Gisborne's sword on his own, sweat beaded on his brow, and his face was the same hue as his hair.

Rachel saw disaster about to strike before Will did. She wanted to cry out, but knew that would defeat the purpose of what they'd done. Gisborne aimed his sword at Will's head again, but when the boy ducked this time, he was met with Gisborne's open palm. Will's head snapped back and he staggered, off-balance. With his opponent weakened further, Gisborne spun, kicking Will's knee; this strike was followed up swiftly by another punch to the face. With that final blow, Will collapsed like a puppet whose strings had been cut, and lay unmoving on the ground.

Silence followed. Gisborne remained above the prone Will, his sword pressed against the back of the outlaw's neck. Rachel found herself breathing frantic prayers that he wouldn't decide to make an end to Will then and there. To her immense relief, he stepped back and sheathed his sword. He jerked his head at Will, and some of his men moved forward, dragging the boy off.

Once that had been accomplished, Gisborne turned to Rachel. Gently, he took her from the man, sitting her down on the ground before he went behind her. She looked over her shoulder as he cut through the ropes around her wrists and removed the gag. "Are you well?" he asked her.

She rubbed her wrists, where the rope had dug in uncomfortably. "Thanks to you," she said, raising her eyes to his. It was difficult to remember that he was a villain in his Story when he appeared so dashing and heroic now.

He gave the smallest hint of a smile. "It was my pleasure, milady," he said.

Rachel wasn't quite sure how to respond to that and said nothing. The man, however, was not at a loss for words. Still moving slowly, he took her hand in his and kissed her knuckles to his lips. "I am Sir Guy of Gisborne, my lady," he told her. She tried to ignore the thrill that went up and down her spine and the blush that came to her cheeks. Never before had she been treated like such a *lady*. Or even had someone outside of her family kiss her, even if it was just her knuckles. Who wouldn't want someone as handsome as Gisborne treating them in that way? Even if he was a villain. "Might you honor me with your name?" he asked.

"Rachel Andric," she said. In her struggle to remain aloof and not turn into some sort of melted puddle of stupidity, her real name passed through her lips. Honestly. She couldn't let herself forget what he was. After all, he was a villain, and a short-lived villain at that. Neither he nor Will made it to the end of their Story, dying either before Robin, in Gisborne's case, or just after, as Will had. Gisborne perished at Robin's hand, and Will was cornered and killed shortly after Robin's death.

She had to try and picture them as simply ink on a page instead of real people. Otherwise, the thought of them undergoing those deaths repeatedly would become too painful. It took her a moment to realize Gisborne was addressing her again. "We'll take you back to Nottingham," he said, helping her to her feet. "Then an escort can take you home."

That set off alarm bells in her mind. He couldn't take her home, because her home wasn't even in The Story at all! What was she going to do? A lie rose to her lips. "I—I came here in search of work," she managed. He was never going to buy it, particularly not with the fancy dress she wore.

However, Guy of Gisborne viewed her with some pity. "I can only imagine the circumstances that pushed that," he said quietly. "Never mind that. Come to Nottingham with me, and we'll see if we can't find you some work."

He didn't notice her ashamed silence as he turned to address his men. "Let's go! The Sheriff will be pleased with our catch, and I want to be out of Sherwood Forest before Robin learns what we've done."

Guy led her out of the outcropping and helped her on his horse. She blushed when she wrapped her arms around his stomach to keep herself from falling, but she'd never ridden on a horse before. Particularly not side-saddle, since her dress didn't let her ride like a man easily. Nor had she ever actually ridden a horse before. She watched with some surprise at the callous way the men threw Will over the back of one of the horses, lashing the unconscious outlaw into place. It was so easy to forget their enmity when she was faced with just one or the other. How could two individuals who seemed so kind hate each other so much?

With his back to Rachel, there was no chance of Guy seeing the furious thinking she was working at. The horses set off at a quick gallop, and she grimaced as the horses' hooves slammed into the ground, churning up leaves, dust, and dirt. The faster they went, the less chance she would have of thinking up a plan to free Will Scarlet.

Otherwise, it would be her fault that he died.

Chapter 4: Nottinghamshire

"What do you mean, *he's been captured*?" Robin Hood's voice was tinged with disbelief. "How could none of us have found him before this happened?"

It was the morning after their conversation with that peculiar man the day before. Now fully in possession of their memories of The Story, Robin felt even more afraid for his nephew than he had before. If The Sheriff had the boy executed, he would undergo Final Death! The idea of never seeing his nephew again hurt more than anything he could think of.

Alan shuffled his feet. He, Little John, and Robin Hood were in the corner of the camp, discussing Will's fate in quiet voices. Robin was doing his best to restrain himself. There was no point in making the rest of the men panic until he himself was able to be calm. "He was with a young woman," Alan explained. "They were cornered by Gisborne and Will was holding her hostage. The story is all over Nottingham." He hesitated, and Robin motioned for him to continue impatiently. "The lady. She had curly blonde hair, and the clearest blue eyes you could ever have seen. Many people are calling her more beautiful than Maid Marian."

A retort that nobody could be more beautiful than Marian rose to Robin's lips, but the realization of the young woman's identity stopped him. "I'd know the description of that young woman's eyes anywhere," he snarled. "It's Andric! Rachel Andric. Just as that man said last night. But how could she become so cruel and evil as to do this to Will, when her parents were so good? Yet that man's words seem true thus far."

31

"Yes, but that man cannot be trusted," Alan pointed out. "You know him as well as I do, though his name eludes us. Memories are a fickle business, aren't they?"

"How The Story can keep us with certain memories and take away others is beyond me," Little John commented.

Robin was in no mood for idle commentary. "Blast it, men, we need to think about Will!" he burst out, far too loudly. Some of the Merry Men cast curious looks at them, and Robin swiftly lowered his voice. "The boy is in danger, John, Alan. I can't help but feel responsible for this, somehow. If I hadn't sent the boy off hunting …"

"The time for blame is done," John said. "What matters now is getting the boy back. We should go to Nottingham."

"Go? And do what?" Robin's voice was bitter.

"Get him back!" Alan put in forcefully. "And be back in time to sing a victory song for dinner. Come now, Robin, chin up. We'll bring Will back here. And all the Merry Men will be at your side. We would fight and die to bring our little brother back home."

Robin stared down at his feet before pushing aside the two men. "Robin!" Alan was taken by surprise. "Where the devil are you going?"

Robin didn't even turn back as he mounted his horse. "Gather the men and meet me in Nottingham," he ordered.

"Where are you going?" John asked.

"To have a word with the lady Andric," he snarled, and spurred the horse on before his two men could tell him what a bad idea that was.

.   .   .   .   .

Guy of Gisborne had taken his prisoner to The Sheriff and left Rachel in his own home. It was dwarfed by the massive stone building beside it and made of grey stone. The inside was sparsely decorated and a tiny bit messy. It consisted of only three rooms—the dining room, the kitchen, and what Rachel assumed was his bedroom. The door was closed to the bedroom.

She sat alone at a wooden table, riddled with imperfections and bore evidence that Guy had sat there many a time and dug his knife into the top repeatedly in tense moments. The hubbub from the streets of Nottingham outside gave the indication of a busy city, but the noise was quieted and muffled in the house.

Rachel's every bone ached from the ride on the horse. Inexperienced as she was, the brutal pace Guy had set with his men on their way to Nottingham had made her discover muscles she didn't even know she had. Even sitting in the chair hurt, yet she lacked the energy to stand up.

It had been an exhausting day, made even worse by the guilt she had over Will's uncertain fate. What could she do to stop it? Although she at least knew how to fight with a sword little from her brother and years of practice, that alone wouldn't be enough to rescue the outlaw. She could seek out the Merry Men, but she knew Guy was watching her, and she had no idea where to find the outlaws anyway. She was out of ideas.

Rachel had no idea how long she had sat at the table in a fog of guilt and disappointment. Her train of thought was only disrupted by the sound of the door sliding open cautiously behind her, the hinges creaking just a little bit. At first, she thought it was Guy, but a split second later, she realized he wouldn't be sneaking up on her and stood, swinging around.

A man with a beard stood there, his face dark with fury. "You're an insult to the name of your parents!" he snarled. Rachel's eyes widened when she saw the big rock in his hand.

"W-wait," she stammered, taking a step back. She hit the wall immediately. "I don't understand!"

The man stepped towards her ominously. "You put Will in danger," he snapped. "You'll pay for that!"

Rachel looked about wildly. This was not what she had anticipated when she entered The Story! The bearded man lunged at her and she dove out of the way. The rock slammed into the wall, making a hole in it. Her mouth was dry as she scrambled for the door. "GUY!" she screamed. Not that she trusted him either, but he was a whole lot better than having her skull be bashed in.

"Don't yell for that swine!" the man shouted back at her, goaded beyond control. He blocked her way to the door and raised the rock.

"Oh gosh," was all she managed to say before he slammed the rock into her forehead.

.   .   .   .   .

Guy sprinted down from The Sheriff's keep when he heard the young woman from the forest scream his name. Why hadn't he left her somewhere safer?! But how was he supposed to have known someone would go after her? For some reason, he found himself praying fervently for her safety.

The knight slammed open the door to his home. What he found there shocked him, and for a moment, he couldn't speak. Then, "*Robin Hood?*"

The outlaw swung towards him. Behind him, crumpled in a heap, was Rachel Andric. Guy couldn't even see where she'd been injured, but he could see the rock in Robin's hand, and the red blood on it. "What the devil is wrong with you?" he bellowed at Robin, drawing his sword. "First your idiot nephew takes her prisoner, then you attack her!"

Robin's face paled somewhat. "I didn't—"

Guy lunged across the table at Robin. The outlaw dove out of the way, his rock clattering from his fingers, and made for the door. Guy jumped after him. However, he'd made the mistake of leaving the door open and Robin ran through it. Although Guy gave chase, he couldn't just leave Rachel on the floor like that, and he stopped when he saw Robin get on his horse and ride away.

Silently cursing the outlaw, Guy turned and went back inside his house. He moved to the other side of the table and knelt beside Rachel. Gently, he rolled the young woman on her side. Sticky blood was caked on her forehead. Her skin felt clammy, and she groaned when he moved her. Although she was semi-conscious, she didn't seem exactly coherent. Guy could only hope no permanent damage had been done to the unfortunate young woman. "Blast you, Robin," he mumbled.

Moving carefully, he scooped Rachel into his arms, resting her head on his shoulder. Whoever she was, and why ever she had been in Sherwood Forest, she certainly didn't deserve to be attacked. She groaned again, and he knew he couldn't leave her there. She needed a physician, immediately.

.   .   .   .   .

The dungeon beneath The Sheriff's manor was as dark and uncomfortable as Will remembered it to be. Moisture dripped down the stone walls, the bars were cold to the touch, and rats squeaked in the shadowy corners. Will sat with his back to the wall, staring past the iron bars at the dark corridor beyond. The only light in the dungeon came from the small, square, barred windows about eight feet from the floor.

Drip. Drip. Will decided that he would go out of his mind from the slow, melodic sound of dripping water long before they executed him. Heaving a sigh, he squirmed, trying to soothe his aching backside. The lumpy stone floor was not made for comfort.

Will squirmed and sighed again. He hated being a burden to the rest of the Merry Men, and now they were going to have to come and rescue him. It wasn't going to make Robin very happy, and that was upsetting to Will. He didn't like to disappoint his uncle.

A scream broke through his thoughts. It sounded like the young woman from the forest, yelling for Guy. But why was she yelling? He stood up, grabbing onto the bars and hauling himself up to the window. All he had was a minimal view of the street, and he couldn't even see any of the houses. Then he heard crunching feet on the gravelly streets and saw Gisborne's lower torso. A hand draped down—a female hand. It was limp.

Will felt a cold hand clutch at his heart. Had someone attacked Lady Andric? If so, why? From his point of view, she had seemed harmless enough. But then, the men had always told him he was naïve, particularly with strangers ...

Sighing, Will released the bars and let himself fall back down to the floor. He sat down heavily. Procuring a pin from his pocket, he proceeded to roll it around his palm, wishing he was good at picking locks. Although he was a thief, the fine art of lock-picking had always been beyond him. Also, the lock on his cell had even flummoxed Robin on a previous occasion. Sighing once more, Will pocketed the pin again. It had been a gift from Robin many years ago, and it meant the world to him. He certainly didn't want Gisborne to find it and take it from him.

About an hour passed, and Will started to doze off in the cell. He used his arm as a pillow, half-conscious, until he heard the door to the manor upstairs open. Assuming it was either a meal or a visitor—the former being a much more appealing option, since none of the Merry Men would dare show their face in Nottingham so flagrantly—he sat up a little.

To Will's shock, the person he'd least expected to see stepped into view—Sir Guy of Gisborne. As the man approached Will's cell, his footsteps rang out in a commanding way, only once differing in sound when he stepped in a puddle of moisture that had dripped down from the ceiling. The man's expression was as inscrutable as ever when he stopped just beyond the bars of the cell and studied Will. The outlaw couldn't help but be extremely curious as to what had brought Gisborne to this dismal and damp place.

Then Gisborne spoke. "The Lady Andric has been attacked. Then she was imprisoned."

"Attacked?" Will could only stare at Gisborne in complete and utter confusion. "By who? And why was she imprisoned? That doesn't make any sense!"

"She was attacked by Robin Hood," Gisborne growled out in a barely-controlled tone of voice. He took a deep breath, mustering an enormous effort to calm himself and control his temper. "Then she was imprisoned by The Sheriff."

Will scratched his head. Neither of those sentences made any sense to him. "You've lost me," he said.

"The Sheriff claims that the Andric family are traitors to the Crown," Gisborne explained, breathing out impatiently through his nose. "And that they are known supporters of the Merry Men."

"I've never even heard her name before, not in all my life," Will disagreed with a shake of his head. "Even I would've heard of her if she was. Robin makes sure we know who all our supporters are."

"I'm sure he does," Gisborne said irritably, but even Will could see he was distracted by his thoughts. He shifted around from foot to foot. Will eyed him carefully, still trying to figure out a point to Gisborne's visit. Finally, Gisborne's gaze came level with Will's, intense yet somehow very desperate. "I have no idea what's going on here. What I do know is that I know that girl's family. I owe her … for something that happened years ago. And I do know that the Merry Men will come here, and they will never leave you to die."

"Most likely," Will agreed. "Am I to be killed?"

"You are to be hung at noon tomorrow," Gisborne said. He hesitated. "You *and* Rachel Andric. My reason for coming here to you is this: I believe that Lady Andric is innocent and does not deserve to die—the exact opposite of you, in fact. I also believe that visitor of The Sheriff's yesterday is responsible for this death sentence that has been placed upon Lady Andric's head."

There was more to Gisborne's reasoning than what he was saying, Will knew it. His words about her family showed that much. Whenever the man spoke the name "Andric", an unmistakable expression would come over his face. Guilt … and regret. The outlaw chose to say nothing, waiting to see if Gisborne would continue.

And he did continue. "If Lady Andric does end up telling me the truth, then I, on my honor as a knight, must take action. If she tells me why exactly she is here, then … something must be done."

38

"Then why are you talking to me instead of her?" Will asked, confused.

Gisborne took in a huge breath, as if it was a physical pain for him to speak the words on the tip of his tongue. "Because ... if I am to rescue her ... then I will need help."

Will blinked. "You ... what?"

"When the time comes ..." Gisborne hesitated again before taking the plunge like a diver jumping off a cliff into the ocean below him. "I'm going to help you escape."

Chapter 5: Honor and Duty

Rachel woke with a low groan. For the second time that day, she couldn't remember where she was or how she'd gotten there. Vaguely, she remembered someone picking her up and carrying her ... somewhere, but that was about it. Her head pounded mercilessly and a cool cloth over her forehead offered some comfort. But who had put it there?

She sat up. A blanket fell away from her shoulders and she found herself in an unfamiliar circular room, devoid of any furnishings aside from the simple bed she was laying in. Sitting on a stool beside her was Guy of Gisborne, looking remarkably forlorn. Rachel focused on him instead of the agonizing pain in her skull. "Wh-where am I?" she asked at last.

"Safe, for the moment," Guy answered. "How do you feel?"

Rachel gave a miserable shrug of her shoulders. "Okay, considering I was bashed over the head," she said. "This isn't your house." She could see out the window, could see that they were quite a way's up.

"No," Guy said, a little reluctantly. "This is the tower prison."

"P-prison?!" Rachel stared at him.

"Tell me the truth, Lady Rachel. Are you truly an innocent? Did Will Scarlet take you prisoner, in the forest?"

The truth spilled from her lips before she could stop it. She didn't know why, but some small part of her trusted him. "I'm not an innocent, and Will didn't take me prisoner. I'm here for a purpose."

Guy seemed amused by her honesty. "Some people wouldn't be so ready to confess that," he said.

"My presence here has nothing to do with the Merry Men, though," she insisted. "Not directly."

"Since it was Robin Hood who hit you, I'd imagine not," he agreed. "Will Scarlet is to hang in twelve hours."

"If it's for what he's done to me, he's innocent," Rachel said, trying to appeal to Guy's better nature.

The man gave a rueful smile. "He's an outlaw, Lady Rachel. Hardly an innocent. I've told him I'd help him escape, but ... only if you tell me the truth. Why are you here?"

Rachel went to answer but stopped. Her training as a Guardian had dictated without question that she should never tell a member of The Story who and what she was. Even if she'd never finished it. And even if it had only been taught to her by her parents and Ewan until they were ... gone. In their memory, she had to keep silent. In a significantly smaller voice, she said, "I'm sorry. I can't tell you."

Anger darkened Guy's face. "Why?" he burst out. "If you are innocent in this, you will tell me the truth!"

Somehow, his anger only served to infuriate Rachel as well. "I don't have to prove my innocence to you!" she snapped. "Because what I'm doing is for you, for all the people here ... can't you just accept that? Can't you do as you told Will you would, and help us both?"

Guy stood up, upsetting the stool and sending it crashing to the floor. "This is a matter of honor to me," he retorted. "You are asking me to betray everything I've ever known, for a young woman who has just admitted to lying to me, and rescue a boy I've always considered my enemy."

"You had the idea of rescuing Will, not me," Rachel said flatly. "Are you going to do it or not? It shouldn't have anything to do with me."

"It has *everything* to do with you," Guy said, obviously making a huge effort to remain calm. "The Sheriff has ordered that you be hung following Will Scarlet."

The news staggered Rachel and she just stared at him. Now his reasoning made sense. The gallant, knightly part of him wanted to stop her from being executed, while the honorable part that was bound to serve The Sheriff didn't think he should. With her concealing what she truly was from him, it was making it harder on him to make the choice.

For a moment, Rachel considered telling him the truth, but duty reasserted itself once again. Just as he had his own code to hold up, she did as well.

"Just ... just tell me," Guy said, his voice pleading.

"I'm sorry," Rachel said, forcing her own tone to be cold. "I can't. My own duty stops me as well."

Fury darkened his handsome face and he turned away from her. "Then let your death and Will Scarlet's be on your head alone," he snapped back at her.

She scrambled out of the bed after him just seconds too late. He slammed the door of the prison shut behind him, and she heard the lock slide home. Too exhausted to go back to the bed, she leaned against the wooden door, her palms pressed against it. She could hear Guy on the other side, doing the exact same thing. "I'm sorry," she whispered to him.

A response came after only a moment. "I am too." Then his footsteps receded and he was gone.

.   .   .   .   .

Alan and Little John were waiting for Robin in the poorer section of Nottingham. Their leader met them there and he cast about for the rest of the Merry Men. "Where have they all gotten off to?" he asked, evidently agitated.

"At ease, Robin," Alan said soothingly. "We've got plans to meet here tomorrow morning. All of us crammed into an alley might attract some attention, hm? Now, where have you been off to? There's a lovely lady here in Nottingham who could use some serenading from her dearly beloved."

Robin glared at Alan, already too incensed to be in a mood for his joking. "Focus, Alan!" he snapped.

"Robin," John said, his deep voice rumbling around. "Where were you? And what the devil is wrong with you?"

Robin knew they would disapprove of what he'd done—to be honest, in hindsight, it hadn't been his best idea. But he couldn't conceal it from them. "I ... I went after the lady from the forest. The one they're saying Will held hostage."

"You went *after* her?" Alan's eyebrows shot up. "As in, went after to her to ask for her help or ...?"

"I ... may have hit her over the head," Robin admitted softly. "With a rock."

"Hit her ... with a *rock*?" Alan shook his head in bemusement. "By heaven, Robin! Don't you know anything about the word 'gallantry'? Or etiquette? The first rule of etiquette is to *not* go around hitting the fairer sex in the head with a rock!"

Little John chuckled. "This is no laughing matter," he reprimanded Alan, still laughing a little.

"Indeed it is not," Robin snapped, stone-serious. "Will's life is at stake!"

That brought a sobering end to Alan and John's amusement. The two exchanged worried looks—they all considered Will to be like their younger brother. The thought that his life was in danger was sobering indeed. "Well, what do we do?" Alan asked.

Robin shrugged. "I just don't know."

"You *don't know*?" Little John's eyebrows shot up. "Since when does the famous Robin Hood not know what to do? What is the matter with you?"

Since John wasn't usually the type of person to be so judging with Robin, the leader of the Merry Men turned to him with wide eyes. But John wasn't finished yet. "You need to think, Robin!" he said flatly. "Will could die, yes. But think about it not as a matter of life or death—think of it as one of our usual heists. But this time, we're stealing Will instead of money."

Robin took a deep breath to calm his nerves. "You're right, of course," he said. He cleared his head of all thoughts of what the man had told him the night before and Rachel Andric. They no longer mattered; it was only Will who did. He owed it to his nephew to rescue him, no matter how he'd gotten captured in the first place. "Right. Here's what we'll do…"

.   .   .   .   .

It was several hours after Guy had left Rachel alone, and she was still exhausted. Unable to sleep after being told she was marked for execution, she had paced the floor of her prison more times than she could count. What would her parents do? Even more importantly, what would *Ewan* do?

At any moment, she knew she could escape. Guardians possessed the ability to make "Story doors"—doors that would take a Guardian from Story to Story. They could also manipulate The Story to perform magic, like causing tremors or unlocking doors. But to run now would mean abandoning Will to Final Death, and she blamed herself for his predicament twice over. First when she had let him hold her hostage and he'd been captured, then again when she had

44

refused to tell Guy what she was and what she wanted to do. Guy would have helped if she had told him, but she'd lost her chance.

Should she have told him? Something peculiar was going on in Sherwood Forest that was going against their planned Story. The Sheriff should never have recognized the name of Andric. Her surname was the only reason the man would have had to imprison her, but he shouldn't have known it unless … unless the intruder had informed him of it, and The Story as well. But what did he stand to gain from doing so?

Finally, restless, Rachel sat down on the bed again. Her mind refused to calm itself, and she struggled to decide what to do. Chances were, Guy wouldn't come back after the argument they'd had. There was no chance that he would come back after her solid refusal to cooperate. What could she do now? There was a guard outside her door, and they had taken her sword from her.

Perhaps it would be in her better interest to leave. But then, what if the intruder was still in Nottingham and did more damage? It would be bad enough if Will underwent Final Death. What about Robin Hood? That would result in an even worse situation. If the main character of a Story were to undergo Final Death, the entirety of the characters of that Story would follow. In other words, she couldn't leave. Not until she knew the intruder was gone and the Merry Men were safe.

Which brought her back to the problem at hand: how to save Will Scarlet. Unarmed, with an aching head, and inexperienced, she had no idea where to start.

She must have fallen asleep, because the next thing she knew, the door to her prison was closing with a thud. She sat up just to find a sword pointed at her. "Stay where you

45

are," said the owner of the sword. "Until we get to know each other a little better."

Rachel recognized him from their earlier confrontation as well as her own books. "Robin Hood?" she said. "Why in the world are you attacking me? And how in the world did you get past the guard?"

Robin kept the sword pointed at her neck. "You caused my nephew to be placed in danger," he said quietly. "I pray that was by accident. As for the guard, getting past them is remarkably easy. All you have to do is tell them you're relieving them from watch and they'll do anything you say."

Rachel met his eyes frankly, deciding to ignore the part about the guard. She supposed being a master outlaw would enable him to lie easily to a simple guard. "I had no intention of putting Will in danger," she said. "He picked me up off the ground and tended to me when I was unconscious. Guy found us, and he concocted the plan to save me."

"Of holding you hostage?" Disbelief was overwhelming on Robin's face. "Not one of his best ideas." Slowly, he lowered the blade. "I believe you."

"Couldn't you have believed me *before* you smashed a rock into my skull?" she asked irritably. "Anyway, we need a plan. Your nephew is going to be executed—"

"At noon tomorrow, I know," Robin said. "And we have a plan. Will you help us, Lady Andric?"

"Why do you want my help?" she questioned.

"Because ..." He took a deep breath. "I knew your parents. I know that you are a Guardian of The Story."

Chapter 6: Execution

There was a large crowd for Scarlet's execution the following day at noon; sadistic fools, the whole lot of them, in Guy's opinion. However much he despised the Merry Men and their utter lawlessness, public executions never failed to disgust him. The bloodthirsty monsters who turned up to watch the unfortunate victim hang should have been on the gallows themselves. However, The Sheriff had insisted that the execution be a public affair, and Guy wasn't powerful enough to overthrow him. Not yet, but eventually, he would be Sheriff.

The Sheriff himself wasn't present for the execution. More than likely, he was hiding in his manor from the sharpened head of Hood's arrow, waiting for Robin Hood to fall into the trap they'd laid to catch him trying to rescue his nephew. Then, once Hood was apprehended, The Sheriff would emerge and proclaim that "his" master plan had succeeded, when it had really been Guy's idea to lay the trap itself. Infuriating.

A glance upward at the tower prison revealed the Lady Andric, standing beside the window. Her refusal to reveal what she wanted in Nottingham made her seem suspicious, but did she really deserve to be hung like a common criminal? As far as Guy knew, she hadn't even done anything that was against the law. From what he had gathered, The Sheriff was only executing her on the word of his burly visitor from two days ago and the fact that he recognized her surname.

A large crowd was gathering already, even though Scarlet's execution wasn't for another hour. Sadistic fools, he thought again. They probably would have wanted to witness the beatings The Sheriff had ordered Will Scarlet to endure as well. However, that was a private matter for The Sheriff's enjoyment alone.

.   .   .   .   .

Robin had departed the previous day after they had enacted their plan, and he had returned only minutes before. Rachel viewed the growing crowd with fury in her heart. "Monsters," she hissed.

Robin shrugged. "They're probably just glad it's not them with the noose around their neck." When she turned, she saw his attention was focused on the bow he was stringing. Once he'd finished, he went to approach the window.

Rachel's exclamation swiftly stopped him. "Don't!" she said. "If Guy sees you up here, he'll know you're here to rescue Will!"

Embarrassed, Robin stepped back. "Right," he said. "I knew that. It's just ... this waiting is driving me mad."

Rachel had spent most of her life on her own; the waiting didn't bother her nearly as much. It was the concern that The Sheriff's men would discover Robin that was worrying her. "Have patience," she advised. "Your men know what to do. You just have to trust them enough, and yourself." He had the most difficult part of the whole plan. If he failed, Will would be hanged and killed, or worse, impaled on his uncle's own arrow.

Robin shifted uneasily. "I know," he said softly, his face paling a little. "I would trust them with my life."

"Then trust them with Will's," Rachel said simply.

Robin looked at her, a frown crinkling on his brow. "You remind me so much of your mother," he told her thoughtfully. "She had the same no-nonsense way about her. What happened to her?"

"She's dead," Rachel answered flatly. "Father, too."

Robin recoiled. "I'm sorry. I didn't know." Then an even-harder question. "What about your brother?"

Rachel let her gaze slide away from his. That was not a conversation she needed to get into at the moment. "He's gone," she said. That was the extent of how far she wanted that particular conversation to go. "I'm going to make sure they aren't bringing Will out." She went to the window, ignoring the bemused look Robin was giving her.

.   .   .   .   .

An hour later, Will Scarlet was dragged onto the gallows, his hands bound behind his back, forced to stand on the platform beside Guy. His ginger hair was sticky with blood from a particularly vicious beating. His back was likewise torn open, and he walked with a distinct slump to his shoulders. The murmuring crowd was silenced when Guy draped the noose around the boy's neck. "You were supposed to help me," Will hissed at him.

Guy shook his head. "I considered it. But things have changed. Our interests no longer align."

"Liar," Will snarled. "Traitor."

Guy said nothing and cleared his throat for the crowd's attention. He flushed when he realized the sound was unnecessary—the crowd was already silent as the grave. Will muttered to him, obviously still angry, "Got a cold, Gisborne?"

Guy felt his eyebrow twitch in annoyance and coughed once to cover his annoyance. "People of Nottingham!" he proclaimed in a loud voice. "Today is a great victory against the outlaw band known as the Merry Men. Today, Robin Hood's nephew, William Scarlet, will hang!" The eerie silence remained unbroken, not even a cheer or a boo. All eyes were locked firmly on them—the executioner beside the victim.

Ignoring the silence, though it sent chills up and down his spine, Guy went to step off the platform. Without warning, something slammed into his forehead, sticky and juicy, and a rotten apple fell to the ground with a soft *splat*. Guy's gaze instinctively shot up, spotting the lanky figure of Alan-a-Dale, the Merry Men's bard, standing in the midst of the crowd with his hands on his hips. "Gisborne, what sort of an ill-bred pig are you, hanging a boy? Didn't your mum teach you any manners?"

Before Guy could send his men after Alan, the bard had ducked back into the crowd and disappeared from sight. Cursing to himself, Guy went down the stairs, distinctly hearing Will mutter to himself, "Alan, you fool, what are you doing?"

"Let the execution commence!" Guy shouted, ignoring the bard's interruption.

. . . . .

Robin jumped up from his seat on the bed of the cell when he heard Guy's shout. "He's going to kill him!" he cried, sounding panicked, and lunged for the window.

"Patience, Robin," Rachel said, despite her own rapidly-beating heart. They had formed a careful plan the night before, and she didn't need Robin's panic messing it up. That was the *last* thing they needed, she knew. "Remember the plan."

"I know that," Robin growled, most likely from nerves more than anything else. He held the bow loosely, the arrow nocked on the thick string.

She prayed that he did. Will's future in The Story—or at any life at all—depended entirely on Robin's ability to shoot at the exact right moment. Too early, and Guy's men would be able to finish Will off before the Merry Men could reach him. Too late and the rope would have snapped his neck. She didn't voice any of her pessimistic thoughts, knowing he had enough to worry about without her adding to his issues.

The crowd outside was deathly silent. Her view from the window was blocked by Robin, and she could do nothing but rock on the balls of her feet in anxious anticipation. "What's happening?" she blurted out. Her nervous couldn't stand it, she had to say *something*.

"He's pausing for dramatic effect," Robin said, his voice tight. Reaching out with his free hand, he eased the window open and leaned on the sill. His grip on his bow was so tight, Rachel feared it would snap beneath his grasp. "Here it comes …!"

.   .   .   .   .

Alan ducked through the crowd, trying to get close to the gallows. Unfortunately, his fury at Guy had gotten the better of him and the throw of the old apple, however satisfying it had been, had ruined his chance at stealth. Soldiers crawled all over the area. Evidently, they were searching for him. But the plan required him to be in place, to back up Little John, and he was too far, and the crowd had already gone silent. Expectation was heavy in the air as they waited for the floor to be dropped from under Will …

The crowd gasped as one as the floor was dropped out from beneath Will. Alan's immediately shot upwards to look at the boy, desperately hoping—*praying*—that their plan had

51

worked. Thank God, the floor had "malfunctioned"—thanks to Much, one of the other Merry Men. Will's foot remained solidly on the platform, but only one, and just barely. If he slipped, he'd fall the rest of the way, and the noose would tighten. Alan began to swear internally as he ran faster, trying to get to the boy before Will's weakness was the end of him. Where was Robin's ... Before he'd even finished the thought, he caught sight of Robin in the window, bowstring snapping forward.

People shoved aside, screaming as Robin's arrow flew through the air. The rope suddenly released, sliced through evenly by the sharp head, and Will tumbled to the wood, falling off the gallows. John was there in a heartbeat. He threw the boy over his shoulder, swinging his quarterstaff liked it weighed nothing with his free hand. The Sheriff's men scattered like pigeons before him. Some were knocked aside by the staff while others fled. But still others dared to stand before him, blocking his path, and Alan was supposed to be there.

Finally, he broke through. Robin was raining arrows down around them. Will hung limply over John's shoulder, unconscious, breathing heavily. Alan drew his sword and pressed his back against John's. "You're late," the bigger man told him.

"Nonsense," Alan answered. "I'm fashionably on time. If I had been late, you would be dead." He punched one of The Sheriff's men in the face and stabbed another at the same time.

John shrugged a little, as much as he could with Will over one shoulder. "True," he agreed. *Crack!* His staff slammed into the skulls of two men at the same time. "Suppose we should be getting off now."

"Suppose so," Alan concurred, as if they were simply saying they were going for a stroll. A cart rolled up on the other side of the square, driven by Much the miller's son, one of the other Merry Men. John and Alan started plowing through the crowd and the soldiers in their attempts to reach it. Robin's hail of arrows had since halted.

.   .   .   .   .

Once John and Alan had driven the men off around them, Robin slung his bow over his shoulder and grabbed Rachel's arm. "Let's go, Lady Andric," he said.

The two of them hurried for the door. Once Robin had thrown it open and pushed her in front of him, they both ran down the stairs together. Rachel's long dress and painful shoes threatened to trip her and send her down the stairs, forcing her to slow her pace somewhat. Robin prodded at her, trying to increase her speed. "I'm going as fast as I can!" she said impatiently, more from nerves than anything else.

They reached the bottom of the stairs without incident. But Rachel was brought to a sudden halt when she pushed open the door at the bottom of the stairs.

Guy of Gisborne and a large group of soldiers waited there for them.

Chapter 7: To Escape

With what was probably an instinctive reaction, Robin grabbed his bow, placed an arrow on the string and aimed it at Guy in one swift movement. "Just what do you think you're doing, Gisborne?" he demanded.

Instead of answering Robin, Guy focused his attention on Rachel. "It would seem that I made an error in trusting you, Rachel Andric," he said in a low voice. "You promised me that you had nothing to do with the Merry Men."

"I said not directly," she said.

Gisborne raised an eyebrow. "Pardon me for mistaking you, then." The sarcasm was practically dripping off his words. "It seems that your word means nothing more to you than a crumb."

"I take offense to that," Rachel said, laying a hand on Robin's arm. He simply stared at her as she forced his bow down. "I never lied to you, Guy. This was the only way I could find to save the most lives."

That brought an annoyed snort from the young man. "Don't play yourself off as the hero," he snapped. "Siding with outlaws is not heroic."

Rachel raised her chin with a touch of pride. "I cannot concern myself with your politics," she said. "I have to set my sights higher, Guy. For the good of everyone—including you."

"For the final time," Guy said, obviously struggling to hold his temper in check. "What is your purpose here?"

She met his eyes frankly. "My purpose here is fulfilled." Something in his expression changed, indicating that he realized, for the first time, that she was telling him the *whole* truth. "You can say what you will now."

There was something a little more hesitant in his face now. Perhaps he truly thought now that she was acting in people's best interest. However, one of his men growled out a question, intruding on the silence between them. "Let's go, men!"

Robin raised his bow as the men charged, but Rachel was faster. As a Guardian, she had access to powers that she rarely used. Now seemed as good a time as any. Reaching deep inside herself, Rachel tapped into all her emotions, something she almost never did. To bring all her grief and anger for her years alone on the Andrics' island invited pain. But emotion was the only thing to activate the spell.

She slammed her fist into the ground, pushing Robin aside as she did so. There was a light rumbling sound, almost like a distant thunderstorm. The rumbling became more fervent and started shaking the castle. Guy's men halted in their tracks. Fear was written all over their faces, and suddenly they didn't look much like they wanted to fight anymore. Unfortunately for them, the spell had been enacted and there was no taking it back now, for better or for worse.

A minor earthquake sprang up at their feet. It hurled them to the ground with a fierce intensity, cracking their heads against the stone floor. Only Guy and Robin were spared from the blow.

Rachel remained bent over, exhaustion assailing her. She had never used the powers before and the tiredness that hit was startling; it took her breath away. Robin, instead of being concerned for her, took a step back. "Sorcery!" he exclaimed with a gasp.

She did her best to glare at him from her doubled-over position. "It's not sorcery," she snapped through clenched teeth. "It's part of a Guardian's abilities. Manipulation of The Story."

"I still say it's sorcery," Robin said, though he didn't look as tense.

Guy drew his sword and pointed it at Rachel. "Witch," he seethed. She was sorely offended, but before she could speak, he lunged at her.

Many things happened in the split seconds that followed. In an instinctive reaction to Guy's attack, Robin brought his bow up to full draw, the feather very lightly touching his cheek. However, Rachel jerked at his arm as he let the arrow fly. The unexpected hindrance caused Robin's aim to go off, Guy's blade switching targets and slicing through the bow as easily as a knife through butter.

It was as Robin jumped back that Rachel heard a peculiar sound. It resembled a galloping horse, but almost seemed heavier than that. With her eyes locked on the hallway behind Guy, she almost got decapitated when he swung the sword at her head. Robin dragged her to safety, yanking her away.

Before Guy could follow up on his advantage, a blur of brown cloth slammed into him. Little John tackled Guy and dragged him down to the floor, punching him as they both fell. When Little John stood up and brushed himself off, Guy was still unconscious on the ground. "You need to watch your back, Robin," the big man said.

"Thanks for watching it for me," Robin answered. "Is Will safe?"

"Safe as he can be with Alan," John said. "We should really go."

Rachel stopped them. "We're taking him." She indicated Guy with a wave of her hand.

As she had expected, the two Merry Men turned disbelieving and horrified faces on her. "Him?" Robin choked out. "Why the devil do you want him?"

They would never understand her reasons, she knew that. By this time, she was aware of the fact that the intruder had been meddling in places he didn't belong. She was smart enough to realize that Robin couldn't have known she was a Guardian if he hadn't been told and reminded of The Story. And if he had finished his mischief in Sherwood Forest and Nottingham, it was a good assumption that he had moved on to ruin other Stories as well.

She would have to follow him, search for him, and stop him. But if he went about recruiting villains, she would have to likewise recruit people to her side. It was no longer a case of damage control. The near-death experience of Will Scarlet had shown that. It was life and death for many of the members of The Story, and she couldn't afford to fail them. Even if it meant declaring war on the intruder himself.

Her reason for wanting to bring Guy was a little more confused. Part of her insisted that it was because she wanted to use him as a sort of test-run—see if she could convince him, and use her persuasion on others later. But the more honest piece of her wondered if it was something more. The way he'd spoken to her, the conversations they'd had ... his inherent nature that seemed to trust her. What caused it? And he'd mentioned something ... something about her parents. A look that passed over his face as he spoke the name of Andric ...

Realizing the Merry Men were still staring at her, Rachel shook herself out of her own thoughts. "I have my reasons," she said in answer to Robin's indignation. "And you owe me. I saved you from Guy's men, remember? And I helped you save Will."

Probably just to appease her and get them moving, Robin nodded grudgingly. "Pick him up, John, so we can get moving. Happy, Lady Andric?"

Rachel gave him a tight-lipped smile. "Oh, of course," she said sarcastically.

After glancing between Robin and Rachel a few times, John shrugged to himself and picked up Guy, tossing him over his shoulder haphazardly. She grimaced inwardly at the way Guy's neck swung around. "Don't snap his neck off," she said.

John glanced at her. "Ahh, it'd take more than that to kill him," he said, brushing her off.

Sighing, Rachel followed the two men out of the manor and into the sunlight beyond. The crowd from the failed hanging was still panicking, allowing the three of them, with the unconscious Guy, to blend in relatively well. It would have been a little better if Little John hadn't been so big, but as of yet, they hadn't been spotted.

That could only have lasted for so long. Rachel heard the sound of shouts of alarm from some of The Sheriff's men, puzzling over the empty gallows. "Go to the cart," Robin ordered, pointing at the wagon at the end of the square. From what Rachel could see, there were only two men in there. She hoped Will was there.

The three of them broke into a run as The Sheriff's men gave chase. Rachel struggled to keep up with the two men, once again hindered by her skirt and painful shoes; she really needed to do away with them. Whether to speed her along or just help her, Robin grabbed her arm, pulling her along with them. She would have appreciated the gesture if it didn't mean Robin was pulling her arm out of its socket.

They reached the wagon and John threw Guy in carelessly before tumbling in after him. After waiting for a brief moment, Robin hauled himself in and grabbed Rachel's arms, tugging her in indelicately and sending her slamming into the bottom of the wagon. "Go, Alan!" he shouted.

Alan jumped up, using the extra leverage to spur the horses on to greater speeds. Rachel, in attempting to rise from the bottom of the wagon, happened to look behind them and spotted a group of men gathering at the other side of the square. The weapons in their hands were raised. "Archers!" she yelled.

With the fury of panic spurring him on, Alan started striking the horses harder. "Move! Hurry!" he cried.

The arrows came back to full draw and fired forward. Horror filled Rachel as she realized that all of them were aimed at one target. Desperation fueled her as she lunged at Alan, wrapping her arms around his knees. "Get DOWN!" she screamed, and pulled as hard as she could, dragging him off the seat of the wagon and into the body itself.

A split second after Rachel had made her move, the arrows struck down into the wood, quivering after they stuck where Alan had been only moments before. Even without anyone to spur them on, the horses shot off, frightened by the loud yells. Little John took the reins and guided them out of the square.

As the wagon rumbled its way out of Nottingham, Alan turned wide eyes onto Rachel. "Milady! I owe you my life," he said with an exaggerated bow from a seated position. Then he sagged backwards against the side of the wagon, a little out of breath.

"You do seem to make a habit of pulling our fat out of the fire." Rachel turned, seeing Will in the wagon for the first time. He had been behind her, slumped over, his face pale, but he smiled at her as he continued speaking. "You have my thanks." She had to hastily avert her eyes when she saw a thin trickle of blood on his hairline, apparently where he'd been struck.

"Alan, what the devil were you doing, standing there like a blasted target?" Robin berated him. "Now I owe her my nephew's life and yours as well!"

Alan jumped up and swept Rachel a graceful bow, despite the jostling of the cart as it rolled off the stones of Nottingham and into the bumpy dirt roads of Sherwood Forest—if the indistinct paths below them could even be thought of as roads. "You have my thanks," Alan said. "I am Alan-a-Dale, bard of Sherwood Forest, soon-to-be father, husband to the most beautiful woman in all of England, and a proud member of the Merry Men!" A particularly harsh bump sent him tumbling down to the wagon, but it didn't dampen his enthusiasm at all. "If you ever want a tune to pull your heartstrings or make you smile, just turn to me and I shall gladly comply."

"For the sake of all of us, please don't take him up on that," Will put in, sending Robin a grin. "Robin might flay him alive. He can go on all night."

"Spare us that, at least," John muttered.

Alan's expression morphed into one of exaggerated and injured dignity. "You just don't understand talent when you hear it."

"Or when we don't hear it," Will answered with an innocent smile.

Before Alan could give voice to anymore protests, Robin interrupted them. "We're almost to the campsite," he said. He contemptuously jerked his thumb at Guy's still-unconscious form. "Someone tie that scum's wrists and ankles," he added. "He's her problem, but he's not escaping to cause us more grief."

Rachel watched impassively as Robin and Alan bound Guy's wrists and ankles together. A third Merry Man, short and slight, who had been previously hidden behind Little

John, came out of hiding to help them. Will leaned over to her. "That's Much," he said. "Robin's closest friend, next to Little John."

"Thanks," she said. The fair-haired man, sensing their attention, blushed a deep crimson and, once he had finished tying Guy's ankles, ducked back behind the protection of Little John.

The wagon rumbled on to its destination of the Merry Men's campsite, and lulled by the motion and the lack of action, Rachel fell asleep.

Chapter 8: Something of a Truce

Rachel woke to chaos all around her. The hubbub seemed to fill her senses, overwhelming her, making her already-aching head pound even harder. For several seconds, she couldn't remember where she was or what was happening. Then one voice, singing as loudly as possible, brought her back to reality and she remembered. The intruder, the Merry Men, the attempted execution …

"Lady Rachel?" It was Robin, kneeling in front of her in the cart. "We've arrived at the campsite."
She nodded her thanks and stood, stretching her fingertips up. Once she had woken herself up a little more, she took the chance to look around from her position in the wagon.
Little John had helped Will Scarlet out of the wagon, lowering him down gently. Immediately, the young outlaw was mobbed by the twenty-odd Merry Men, all speaking loudly and yelling out greetings to him. To add to the hubbub and chaos, Alan had jumped on the side of the wagon, singing at the top of his lungs. Since he was only perched on the small siding of the cart, he ended up falling off, singing the entire way down and as he stood, not even missing a beat. It wasn't that his voice was bad, but it was loud and seemed to be rattling Rachel's skull.

Rachel felt tempted to clap her hands over her ears. After years of solitude, the tumult felt extra loud. A glance over her shoulder revealed that Guy was still tied up, but conscious. He had his eyes squeezed shut and kept hitting his head on the wood behind him on purposely. He looked like he'd rather be dead than at the campsite.

Little John offered Rachel his hand, and after she put her fingers in his palm, he helped her down. Rachel noticed when she was on the ground that every time one of the men clapped Will on the back, the young outlaw grimaced. With some concern, Rachel saw the thin lines of blood on the back of his shirt, knowing that he must have been beaten while imprisoned.

Of all the Merry Men present, Rachel saw two women. One had curly red hair, braided over her shoulder, her dark green eyes scanning the group of men. When they lit on Robin, they fairly started to glow. "Robin Hood!" she exclaimed. "You caused me much grief, you foolish outlaw."

Guy inhaled sharply, leading Rachel to believe that the woman had to be Robin and Guy's love interest, Maid Marian. By the time Rachel looked over at Guy, he had recomposed his features and once again simply looked bored. Now, however, she knew it was just an act.

Robin was not watching Guy, of course. He laid his hand on Marian's cheek tenderly and kissed her. "But I always return to you safely, Marian, my love," he reminded her once they'd parted. Rachel looked away a tad bit uncomfortably.

Through the entirety of the conversation, Alan had continued singing loudly. By that time, the greetings had been said to Will and the men were now irritated with the singer. None of them spoke until Robin, finally turning away from Maid Marian, clapped his hands over his ears. "Alan-a-Dale," he growled. "Would you *please* stop that infernal singing?!"

Alan adopted an insulted expression, but finally stopped his seemingly-never-ending signing. "Uneducated pigs don't understand the finer arts of life," he muttered under his breath.

Will, chuckling, slung his arm over Alan's shoulders soothingly. "Come along, old friend," he said. "Let's take your wounded ego over to a fire, shall we? My poor stomach is practically empty." The two moved off together, and most of the Merry Men followed, along with the second woman.

By the time the men had gone off, Marian had spotted Guy tied up in the wagon. "Robin!" she said reproachfully. "Why did you kidnap Sir Guy?"

"I didn't!" Robin insisted, his voice rising a tiny bit. "Lady Rachel and Little John did."

Maid Marian turned her disapproving gaze on Rachel, narrowing her eyes. In response to the disapproval, Rachel raised her eyebrows at the other woman. "And why, 'Lady Andric', did you abduct a key officer of Prince John, and bring him here, where he could exact revenge on all his enemies?"

Rachel squared her shoulders, not looking away. "Normally, I wouldn't have," she said. "However, things have changed. The Story is changing."

Those present went silent. Even the Merry Men at one of the numerous campfires around the clearing went silent, listening. She glanced at Robin, seeing his eyes widen. "What do you mean?" he asked finally.

"None of *this*," she waved her hand around, "was ever supposed to happen. Will was never supposed to come that close to death. Guy was never supposed to corner you, Robin. That should never have come to pass. I should know—I've read your Story often enough."

"I don't understand," Robin said.

Rachel folded her arms, deep in thought. "I failed in my duty," she admitted, her voice soft. She didn't know why, but she told them everything, from the moment when she'd discovered the intruder was on the island to that moment. It was so quiet, even the animals seemed to have gone silent. Never one for being the center of attention, Rachel blushed, trailing off at the end of her tale with a, "And now we're here."

"So we are," Robin answered thoughtfully. He was the only one to speak. Everyone else had thoughtful expressions on their faces, even Guy, from his position in the cart. "How do you intend to get The Story back on track, then? I trust you know that the 'intruder' fellow came to see us, which is why I thought that ... you know ... you had arranged for Will to be caught."

"Is that why you hit her over the head?" Guy asked with a vindictive overtone, probably guessing that Robin was purposely neglecting to mention that.

"Robin Hood, did you do that to her?!" Marian demanded, pointing at the bump on Rachel's forehead.

"Alright, stop! Please!" Rachel waved her hands, trying to get their attention again. "The intruder came to see you?"

"What did he look like?" Guy interrupted, serious once again.

Robin sent him a glare, but Guy returned the sneer with an innocent look. "Please," Guy added.

The outlaw leader frowned. "Fine. He was rather tall, a burly fellow, and had a gravelly sort of voice. In fact, he looked a little familiar ..." His voice trailed off, but the thoughtful frown remained.

"Why?" Rachel asked Guy. His curiosity had to be there for some reason.

Guy inclined his head to the side. "He came to see me," he explained. "Or, more appropriately, he came to see The Sheriff. I only saw him briefly."

"Why would he go and see The Sheriff?" Marian questioned.

"Probably to lay the trap for Scarlet," Guy supplied. "The Sheriff sent me out to find him not thirty minutes after they concluded their conversation. It's my guess that the man informed The Sheriff of Will's position and sent me out to capture him. Which I did."

Before another argument could break out between Guy and Robin, Rachel swiftly interrupted. "It doesn't matter," she said. "What we need to figure out is what to do next."

"We?" Marian replied. "How is this our problem?"

"Marian—" Robin began.

The woman held up her palm towards him to forestall his protests. "Robin, I know you want to help her. But getting involved in a foreigner's problems shouldn't be something you do. We're simply putting ourselves in danger for someone we hardly know. And for what reason?"

"To avoid Final Death." Rachel kept her voice pitched quietly, but with as much insistence as she could put into it.

Alan and Will had rejoined them, the bard's ego seemingly healed. Will's mouth was full of bread, but Alan spoke for them. "Final Death?" he repeated. "You must be joking."

Rachel shook her head. "If The Sheriff is helping the intruder, then you can bet that The Sheriff was promised something. And what better than Final Death?" She pointed at Robin. "No more Robin Hood, no more Merry Men. Isn't that the world The Sheriff always wanted? No outlaws, no problems, right? Final Death is permanent. Irreversible. Final Death for the Merry Men would be The Sheriff's paradise."

The silence that fell over them was hard and smothering. Even Rachel felt uncomfortable, but she forged on regardless. She had to get them on her side. "And it wouldn't end with just you and the Merry Men. Think about it. There are hundreds of Stories in The Story Book. You can't pretend not to know that. The intruder won't get many heroes on his side. Mostly villains. And do you know what will happen to anyone who opposes him? Final Death for all of them. Do you really want that, Robin Hood? For all those people to undergo Final Death, because you refused to act?"

"Enough!" Furiously, Robin clapped his hands over his ears. "I will help. You didn't have to make that speech to me. I *know* the consequences. Don't try and preach to me. But what would you have us do? If this intruder fellow is done here in Sherwood Forest, there's no way we can reach him."

Rachel blew her hair out of her eyes. "First of all, keep yourself safe. If you die, your Story dies with you. As a main 'character', your death would result in the Final Death of everyone here." She waved her hand at all of them. "Secondly, if the intruder is doing what I think he's going to, then I'm going to have to mirror him."

"Recruit villains?" Alan asked in a confused way.

"No. Recruit *heroes*," Rachel corrected him. "You, the knights of the Round Table ... as a Guardian, I can trace his Story doors."

"His Story whats?" Will questioned, looking as confused as Alan.

"Doors. They're the way Guardians travel between Stories. Doors that appear and seem to go to nowhere, until you go through them," Rachel explained. "It's the only way of going between The Story's 'pages'."

"Why would you want to trace his doors?" Little John said.

The many, many questions were beginning to make Rachel's head spin. She forced herself to concentrate, not wanting to miss any of them. "I have to follow him and stop whatever damage I can," she answered. "Save as many lives as possible. And recruit them to my cause, if I can. Even if I can't, they still deserve to survive. Don't they?" She added the last part in a harsh tone, looking directly at Marian.

To the woman's credit, she looked ashamed. "I didn't know. I'm sorry."

Rachel nodded a little. "That's what brings me to all of you. I need you on my side. Otherwise, I … if I can't convince you, what hope do I have?"

"You've convinced us already, Lady Andric," Robin said fervently. "But I think we need some sort of a plan, don't you?"

She nodded slowly. "There's going to be just one way I can get rid of him," she stated. "I have to write him out of The Story."

"I thought people could only be written in," Alan argued, his brow puckered in thought. Rachel was mildly impressed with the argument, though it was mostly annoying for the interruption. Someone must have filled the Merry Men in on the workings of The Story a long time ago. She wondered who it had been …

Trying to maintain her hold on her patience, she shook her head. "No. If a Guardian goes to The Heart of The Story, they can write the name of any person in The Story Book there and write that person out."

"And … what happens to them then?" Will questioned.

"I don't know. Maybe they die. Maybe it's Final Death. Or maybe they're just banished from The Story." Rachel shrugged helplessly. "I'm a junior Guardian. I'm not privy to that sort of information."

"What information *are* you privy to?" Little John wondered aloud.

Rachel shrugged. "Unfortunately, not the location of The Heart, or how one is supposed to rewrite The Story. If it was easy, the intruder could've done it himself."

"So there's some sort of trick to it," Alan guessed.

She nodded. "I assume. So I'll also be looking for Guardians in The Story—one who can tell me what I have to do." Perhaps one Guardian in particular ...

"I thought Guardians only came in The Story to fix certain things," Robin said with a frown.

"If a Guardian makes a mistake, they—they're written into The Story as one of the characters," Rachel explained, her voice falling into a mumble. "I'm hoping to find an experienced Guardian who's actually been in The Story before."

"So while you're larking off after this intruder, what do you want us to do?" Robin asked. "I'm sure you don't want all of the Merry Men trailing after you."

"No, of course not." She knew how they were going to react, but she said it anyway. "I need an army. There's going to be a battle at The Heart, I know there is. He's gathering people like The Sheriff to his side for a reason. What I have to do is make sure that he doesn't get there before me. So I need people to fight him and make sure he doesn't have a bigger army than me. At least, not a *much* bigger army ..."

"You want all of us to undergo Final Death?" Robin cried. "Are you mad? Fighting him will only result in that!"

"That's not true," Rachel argued, putting her hands on her hips. "Without working with me, the intruder will most certainly force you to undergo Final Death. All of you. *But*, if you fight with me, as my army ... yes, some of you will die in battle, and yes, it will be Final Death. However, if I can get to The Story Book at The Heart in time, I can restart The Story's cycle so your Final Deaths never happened. There's a brief, twenty-four hour period when Final Death can be reversed. Anyone who dies during the battle will return when I reach The Heart and fix this mess."

"You might need help, going through The Story like that," Will commented. When she glanced over at him, she noticed that his cheeks were bright red and he wouldn't meet her eye. "He'll probably send people after you, too. I-if you'd have me ... I'd like to go with you." Even with his words out in the open, he still refused to look up, and shuffled his feet. It was evident that he expected to be refused.

"Wouldn't you rather stay with the Merry Men?" Rachel asked with a frown. She hadn't expected any of them to offer their company and aid directly.

Will looked up without warning, his dark eyes intense. "I want to help," he said. "And I think I'd be of more use to you than staying here, twiddling my thumbs until you call us."

Rachel was torn. As much as she wanted some help on her quest, she knew that anyone who came with her would be more at risk than if they stayed behind. She'd had half of an idea to ask Guy to come with her, but her fear of putting him at risk had forced the idea away. Now Will's offer of help was bringing out her concerns once more. She worried that she couldn't protect them well enough and that one or both would perish because of her.

Robin must have sensed her indecision, for he hastened to interrupt Will before the boy could speak. "Though he's only sixteen, he's as good a fighter as all the rest of us—aside from John," he added, when Little John opened his mouth to protest. "And he's an excellent shot with a bow, as well as being a spot-on archer. He may not have the greatest sense of direction, but he's level-headed and reliable. You couldn't ask for a better companion."

70

"You saved my life, Lady Andric," Will pressed on with a hint of desperation. "I need to repay that favor to you. Please."

Deciding to give it a try, Rachel sighed. "First of all, can everyone call me Rachel, please? I don't really like 'Lady Andric'. Secondly, Will, I'd be glad to have you, but you've got to understand the risks. Once we leave this Story, you could die. My quest is probably going to be really dangerous, and I wouldn't want you to get ... hurt."

"I'm aware of the risks," Will answered simply. "I want to fight for my home, no matter the cost. Please."

Rachel hesitated for a second more before her face relaxed into a wry smile. "Alright, then. Welcome aboard, Will Scarlet."

Robin stepped forward. "Give yourselves a night's rest before heading out," he suggested. "Friar Tuck can see to your back, Will, and make sure there's no danger from it. You can have a good rest, and we'll give you some supplies before you head out."

She nodded before turning back to Guy. Since she had committed herself with Will, it couldn't hurt to bring a fully-trained knight along with her too. "I trust you have no problem if Guy comes with us too, Will?"

"*Gisborne?*" Every single one of the Merry Men gave the same startled exclamation. Robin added, "Why the devil would you want Gisborne to come with you?"

She squared her shoulders. "Guy?" she said.

He looked up at her. "Everyone in this Story will die, if Robin Hood is to perish before his time?" he questioned. She nodded. "Much as I hate you, Hood ... I do not want everyone to undergo that fate because of you. I will pledge my aid to you, Lady—Rachel."

Rachel climbed back into the wagon a little awkwardly and extended her hand towards Robin, palm-up. Reluctantly, the outlaw placed a knife into her palm and she cut Guy loose. After he was free, she reached out to help him up. "Welcome to the group," she told him. Then, after hauling him to his feet, she turned back to the Merry Men. "Let's have something to eat."

Chapter 9: Final Night in Sherwood

That night, the Merry Men held a going-away feast for
Will. After Friar Tuck had declared the boy fit for travel, they
had proceeded to go hunting and brought back a deer.
Although Rachel cringed a little and looked away when they
skinned it, the men treated the meal with the utmost respect.
Ale was broken out and Alan started to sing—a little more
seriously than when he'd originally done so as they had
arrived. The brown-haired woman with her hand on his
shoulder was his wife and evidently several months pregnant.
He sat in the midst of the men, stroking his lute and going
between singing jaunty country songs to low-key, sad ballads.
Most of the time, when he tried to sing the ballads, the men
would berate him into switching into something a little more
upbeat.

Despite the Merry Men's complaints, Alan's singing
was actually quite good. Rachel sat apart from the outlaws,
leaning against a tree, listening. In the relative peace of the
moment, she reflected that many Guardians should have seen
what she was witnessing now. From conversations she'd had
with her brother Ewan and her parents, she knew that most—
if not all—Guardians thought of The Story members as
characters, ink on a page, so to speak. But now, seeing the
men celebrating Will's safe return, yet at the same time,
quietly dreading the moment when he would leave, she could
see. Clearly, she could see.

The emotions—both the ones the men demonstrated
and the ones they hid—were so completely human that
Rachel knew that they weren't just words on a page. Their
fears, their love, their sadness ... they were people. They
deserved to *live*. For the first time in her life, she began to

understand why Ewan had done what he did. *I know why you left me now. I understand. If only I could tell you that ...*

Her thoughts were interrupted when Guy of Gisborne sat down beside her. He had a piece of meat that he extended to her. "Friar Tuck said you should eat," he said.

She accepted the venison with a little smile. "Thanks," she answered.

They both fell silent for a few minutes, listening to Alan's music. Robin had his arm around Will's shoulders, laughing with the boy, who was turning a bright red. Guy was staring down at his lap. "You're probably wondering why I offered to help you," he said quietly. "After I called you a traitor and liar."

Rachel shrugged, swallowing her bite of venison. "I assumed it was for the reason you told us. That you didn't want anybody to die and that you were willing to put aside any of your past grudges. And isn't it?"

Guy's gaze slid away from her, giving her an answer. "There's more to it," he admitted. "It's—you, Rachel. Something about you. You're a Guardian. I did something, once, something I greatly regret. I feel I must make it up to you. And that you're just ... you. I suppose. What I mean is, you command attention. Everything you do—it's like you're completely confident, even when you're terrified inside. There's just something about you."

Rachel's eyebrows shot up. "I thought I lied to you and betrayed your trust," she reminded him.

"You did. However, once I heard your tale, I realized why you couldn't be honest with me," Guy answered. "I would have thought you were insane or reported you immediately to The Sheriff. But giving you the chance and hearing you out, I realized that you ... what you're doing is entirely unselfish. I'm doing it because I don't want the innocent to die with the guilty. Will is helping because he wants to protect his family. Why are you doing it?"

Rachel looked away. "For my family," she said. "Family and duty. Duty is all I have left."

"You look like your mother." From the irritated expression Guy's face, she gathered that he hadn't intended to say that. "I ... I mean ..." He was floundering. "I just—"

"You knew my mother?" Rachel asked softly.

He ran a rueful hand over his face. "I knew your mother," he admitted. "Well, more appropriately, I crossed paths with your mother, and your father, I assume. Your mother's face just resembled yours entirely. Although she had black hair, her eyes ... *your* eyes ... I can't seem to lose the image of them."

Rachel picked at her dress, making another mental note to change it into something more appropriate for a quest. "My parents died here, in Sherwood Forest," she said softly.

Guy stood up abruptly. "My condolences," he said. "Then it's possible that I saw them just before they died. I need to rest before tomorrow. Good night."

Confused by his sudden turn of mood, Rachel gave a confused "Good night," as he walked away. Alone once again, she leaned back, finishing off her venison. Inwardly, she laughed at herself. For someone who couldn't even look at the deer getting skinned, she hadn't put up any sort of fuss about eating it. Then again, she hadn't really had anything to eat in two days.

She made herself more comfortable, finding that she had no reason for a cloak. The autumn air was cool, but not freezing, and her dress provided enough warmth. The Merry Men continued celebrating for several more hours until Will announced that he was exhausted. Alan jumped to his feet, upsetting his mug of ale. "Then a final song, to serenade our hero!" he proclaimed.

Rachel would have expected the serenade to be upbeat and rather militaristic. What she was *not* expecting was a soft, quiet ballad, played on Alan's lute with absolutely no vocal accompaniment. It seemed to sweep through the clearing, even dimming the leaping flames of the five campfires. The haunting melody came like a cold wind, sending shivers down the spines of all those present. Alan's gentle hand on the strings of the lute plucked out complicated chords that came out simply. The eerie strains seemed to set the Merry Men ill at ease. From her position on the outskirts of the captivated audience, Rachel could see tears lingering in their eyes; no matter what they said or did, most of them were fearful sending Will away, where they couldn't help him.

A bit of guilt crept into Rachel's heart. She was taking Will away from them. The thought made her even more concerned that something was going to go wrong. If something happened ... if Will *died* ... how could she come back and tell these men? His family? And it wouldn't be anyone's fault but her own.

The song drew to a close. Nobody applauded—in fact, the strange spell that had fallen over them seemed to continue as they all drifted off to sleep. Alan looked vaguely offended, but his wife drew him away before he could complain. While most of the men skirted around Rachel, Will surprised her by sitting down next to her. "He does that," he said, motioning after Alan. "He likes to end on a low note. He says it makes him different from other performers." The boy gave a little snort of amusement. "I think he just likes to show that he can make grown men cry."

"Alan's very talented," Rachel said, not really sure if that was what Will wanted her to say.

He laughed. "I suppose he is. But the men never really give him much of a chance to sing," he said. "They don't really like to show off their sentimental side. Ellen satisfies his desire to perform, though."

"His wife?" Rachel guessed. She couldn't remember her name from the legends.

Will nodded. "His wife. She was originally supposed to marry one of Gisborne's fellow knights, but she branded herself an outlaw to marry Alan instead. I wanted to thank you," he added. "For helping to save me, and Alan too."

Rachel shrugged a little. "It was the best thing I could do, since it was probably my fault you got captured in the first place."

That made Will laugh. "Your fault?" he repeated. "How the devil was that your fault? It was my own fault for getting lost and my idiotic plan to hold you hostage. I should've known that Gisborne would never fall for it."

"It wasn't Guy that was the problem," Rachel said. "The Sheriff somehow knew my family name."

Will grinned crookedly. "So, basically, it was *neither* of our faults?" he said. "Let's just blame it on The Sheriff and move on. It makes things much easier, doesn't it?"

Rachel couldn't help it. She covered her mouth and started laughing. "It does," she agreed, still trying to smother her giggles.

The two of them sat together for a little while longer in companionable silence. Finally, Will stood up, but he didn't leave quite yet. Instead, he looked back at Rachel, shifting from foot to foot. "I wanted to thank you. For letting me come with you," he said after a long moment.

"Thank me?" Rachel met his gaze, confused. "Why should you thank me when you're the one who's coming to help me?"

"For giving me a chance to prove myself," Will said, meeting her eyes firmly. "I made a lot of mistakes when I first joined the Merry Men. I hope to make it up now by becoming a hero and save them from a terrible fate."

"We might not be heroes," Rachel pointed out.

Will gave her a smile. "That's where you're wrong, Rachel. You saved my life, and Alan's. That makes you a hero in my eyes."

Before she could protest or even react, the outlaw had walked away. Since everyone else was already sleeping, Rachel could do nothing but lay down and do the same. She stared at the sky for a while, realizing that she was sleeping under the stars for the first time in her life. To the sounds of insects buzzing in the trees and an owl hooting somewhere, her eyes drifted closed and she fell sound asleep.

Chapter 10: Red

The morning after Alan's performance went by quickly. Most of the farewells had been said the night before, and the breakfast hours were devoted to making sure Rachel, Will, and Guy were properly prepared—though mostly Rachel and Will. Food was packed into satchels, medicinal supplies, each was given a sword, and Rachel was even given breeches and a tunic. They were a little big, but much better than her dress, and considering that she had never used her Guardian ability to change her clothes before, now was not the best time to be experimenting with them.

Once they were properly supplied, most of the men drifted away with a clap to Will's shoulder or a grim shake of the hand. Alan eschewed their grimness and gave Will a hug, ruffled his hair, and told him to "Come back soon, little brother," before backing off. Will sent him a slightly-trembling smile.

It was Robin who approached him last. He gripped the boy's forearm, and Rachel, watching from the side, saw tears in both of their eyes. Without warning, Robin pulled him into an embrace. "Stay safe, Will," he whispered. "I can't lose you like I lost your mother."

"I'll be careful, Uncle," Will answered in the same tone. They remained in that position for several seconds before Will finally pulled away. "I guess we'd better get going, then."

"Guess so," Robin said. He rumpled Will's hair affectionately before stepping back. After one more moment of looking at his nephew, he turned and bowed slightly to Rachel. "You two come back in one piece, alright?"

"Will do," Rachel replied. "Ready, Will? Guy?"

Guy, who looked like he'd rather be anywhere in the world other than at the campsite, nodded. "I've been ready," he said.

Will reddened somewhat but didn't rise to the bait. "Ready," he said.

Rachel closed her eyes, extending her senses to trace the intruder. A Story door had recently been made to leave Sherwood Forest. With just a little bit of effort, she connected to that door and forced open one of her own. It wasn't something she'd done in The Story before, but all Guardians learned how to open one from a young age.

All of the Merry Men drew back with a shocked and terrified gasp. Even Will and Guy looked a little uncomfortable. Rachel had little patience for their fear. "We've already established that I have magic as a Guardian," she said impatiently. "This is basically like turning a page in a book. Robin, thank you for the supplies. I'll send Will back to call you to war."

Robin nodded grimly in return. "Godspeed, Rachel."

"Thank you," she said. With that, she, Guy, and Will departed Sherwood Forest through her Story door.

.   .   .   .   .

When Rachel stepped through the Story door, she was displeased and annoyed to find herself in yet *another* forest. She'd been hoping for someplace that was immediately evident where they were, not another blasted forest. On top of that, their clothes weren't nearly warm enough, and she pulled her cloak closer to herself. She made a mental note to use her magic and make a warmer cloak for herself.

Will and Guy came through the door, and it slammed shut behind them, slowly fading from sight. Immediately,

Will started looking around, his brown eyes wide, obviously trying to absorb as much as possible. With his head whipping to and fro, he resembled an excited puppy.

Guy took a more casual approach to the whole situation. "Where are we?" he asked, keeping his gaze fixed on Rachel. He was possibly trying to not look as curious as Will.

Disguising the sigh that fought to escape her lips, she shrugged. "I'll let you know when we meet someone," she answered.

While Guy gave her an almost frustrated look, Will was wandering around, his eyes scanning the ground. At first, Rachel thought he was just trying to look at foreign ground. Then Guy spoke impatiently. "Scarlet, what the devil are you doing?"

Will looked up. "She said she wanted to find somebody to see where we are," he explained, as if that was obvious. "So I was trying to track someone."

"Track?" Guy gave a snort. "Good luck. The ground's frozen and hard as a rock."

Will assumed a superior look. "Oh, really?" he said. "Then what do you call *that*?" He pointed at the ground with a smile.

Rachel looked at the spot he'd indicated and immediately looked away, blanching. "That's a lot of blood," she said, her voice a little choked.

Looking rather sheepish, Guy said nothing, looking away. The scarlet trail wound its way through the trees, looking as if whoever was bleeding had dragged a limb—presumably their leg—along behind them. Will stood up from his crouched position, meeting Rachel's eyes. "Someone's injured," he said.

"It could be an animal," Rachel suggested. She really didn't want to see the wound that could produce such a tremendous amount of blood. The worst thing in the world for her was blood. She didn't know why, but she couldn't look at it without becoming nauseated. "Or a trap by the intruder. He's here somewhere. We should really—" She stopped as Will started hurrying through the trees, following the trail of blood. "Leave it alone," she finished in a mumble.

Possibly hearing the displeasure in Rachel's tone, Guy turned a puzzled and rather amused expression on her. "He's far too excited over a bit of blood," he muttered with a sigh, but followed the outlaw.

"*That's* a bit?" Rachel eyed the trail for a brief moment before squeezing her eyes shut. "Ugh." Heaving yet another sigh, she pulled her brown wool cloak around her, the air in the forest they were currently in much colder than it had been in Sherwood Forest. On the track ahead of her, she heard voices flare up, one distinctly feminine and unhappy, the other belonging to Will, almost shrill and insistent.

Since it sounded like they were arguing, Rachel picked up speed and broke through the trees. On the dirt indentation that made up the path, a raven-haired young woman was sprawled out, glaring up at Will. The outlaw knelt beside the young woman, pink in the face, while Guy hovered over his shoulder, looking more interested in the argument than the obvious wound in the girl's leg. Blood oozed from gashes in her lower leg, although she was clutching it with her hands. It seeped through her fingers, and Rachel turned, trying to hold on to the small breakfast she'd had before leaving Sherwood.

"Leave me alone," the young woman snapped, a French accent laying heavily on her words. A red cloak lay on the ground beside her, torn by what looked like the briars and thorns of the forest. "I do not need your help!"

Looking petulant, Will crossed his arms and glared at her. "Let me look at it," he said insistently. "If you don't let

82

me treat it now, you could lose the leg, or even your life. Is that really what you want? To die in this forest, bleeding out, for the sake of your blasted pride? Just let me help!"

"Stay away!" the young woman snarled, jerking back. Her dark grey eyes flashed with pain. "I would rather lose the leg than accept help from an Englishman."

"That seems a bit silly," Will commented. "Besides, you're not getting helped by an English*man*. I'm an English *boy*."

Guy gave vent to an impatient sound before grabbing her shoulders and forcing her down to the ground. "I wouldn't normally do this to a woman," he said quietly. "But in this matter ... I think it's excusable."

The French girl wrenched free from his grasp, grabbing a small club off her belt in the process. She then proceeded to beat at Guy's arm, trying to get him to release her. Rachel had to step in and grab the club mid-swing, pulling it from her hand and hastily scooting backwards when the girl scowled at her. "Stop fighting!" Rachel insisted. "He's only trying to help you."

"I do not need help from any of you!" the other girl insisted. However, sweat was gathering on her brow, and her face was growing pale as she weakened from loss of blood.

With Guy still pressing her down to the ground, she could do nothing as Will used a knife to cut the ruined breeches away from her injured shin. The claw marks that had savaged her skin made their way down from the bottom of her knee to her ankle. Bile rose in Rachel's throat, and she hastily turned away. There was just way too much blood.

Once the breeches had been cut away, Will grabbed one of their canteens, pouring some water on a spare scrap of cloth. He proceeded to scrub at her wounds, the large amount of blood seeping from the scratches not even bothering him.

Rachel didn't know how he did it. "Since when were you a physician?" Guy asked, a hint of reluctant approval in his voice.

"Ever since I joined the Merry Men," Will said. "Friar Tuck taught me when I first went to Sherwood Forest." He had a little smile on his face, as if revisiting old memories. However, most of his attention was still devoted to his work on the young woman's leg. She was not at all interested in what he was saying, judging from the scowl on her face, but she seemed to have promised herself that she wouldn't make a sound.

"What exactly clawed you, miss?" Will inquired curiously, ignoring the blood on his hands as he continued to clean the wound.

The girl sent him a glare. "A wolf."

Rachel bent down, picking up the torn red cloak and holding it up. "Is this yours?" she asked, now pretty sure she knew where they were.

"Do not touch that!" The young woman lunged towards Rachel, only held down by Guy. Even then, he grimaced, looking as if he were struggling.

Sensing that she was somehow only making the young woman more agitated, Rachel folded the cloak carefully and laid it down beside the girl. "I'm sorry," she said. Then, a few seconds later, she dared to ask, "Are you Red Riding Hood?" There was just no way that she could be called "little" Red Riding Hood. The young woman had to be somewhere in her early twenties, give or take a few years.

The young woman, Red Riding Hood, eyed Rachel suspiciously. "Ah," she said slowly. "I understand." Just what she understood, she didn't say. Her grey eyes remained locked on Rachel for a few minutes after.

Will broke the silence by tying the knot on his bandage and grabbing a clean cloth to wipe his hands with. "There," he said, with a small amount of pride. "Finished. Friar Tuck would be proud, I think."

Guy eased off Red, and she got to her feet a little unsteadily. He helped her, slipping his arm under her shoulders to support her. Although she looked unhappy, she leaned against him slightly and swayed a fraction. "*Merci*," she said reluctantly, inclining her head to Will a little. Her gaze traveled once more to Rachel. "You—you are a *Tuteur*, are you not?"

Since Rachel, as a Guardian, had to learn all the languages of The Story, she understood what Red was asking. "Yes," she said with a nod. "I'm a Guardian."

"And them?" Red pressed, indicating Will and Guy.

"They're Will Scarlet and Guy of Gisborne," Rachel replied. "I am Rachel Andric."

Red's gaze swung back to her swiftly. "Andric?" she repeated softly. The recognition in her voice made Rachel bite her lip. Just how many Stories had her family gotten themselves involved with?

Finally, Red's piercing stare turned away from Rachel. "Come with me," she said, albeit reluctantly. "I will take you to my home. At least you can eat and sleep for a night or so. It is the least I can do, for what you did for my leg." She indicated herself. "I am Red Riding Hood, as she says."

"Pleasure," Will said, smiling.

Guy inclined his head slightly. "Indeed." There was slight confusion in both of the young men's expressions, no doubt their curiosity at Red's peculiar name. Guy continued on, "We would be most grateful to you for your act of kindness, Lady Hood."

"*Bien*," Red replied awkwardly, which Rachel thought was a rather strange response to what Guy had said. "And ... just call me Red, *s'il vous plaît*. I am no lady."

The two young men nodded once again, and Red gave what probably for her passed as a grin. However, it was only the slightest twitch of her lips upward. "*Merci*," she said again. "Shall we proceed?"

"Yes," Rachel said. There was an unpleasant tingling sensation on the back of her neck, like they were being watched. A glance over her shoulder showed no one in sight, but she continued scanning for several seconds.

There. A flash of black fabric. It was gone in a flash, but it had been there. Swallowing past a lump in her throat, Rachel turned to Guy and motioned for him to pass Red to Will. He must have seen the expression on her face and the backward look, for he obeyed without question. After Red was leaning on Will instead, Rachel saw Guy's hand fall to the hilt of his blade.

Red had her hood tucked under her arm, her raven hair flowing over Will's elbow. It looked a little awkward for them both, considering that they were just about the same height and as long-limbed as the other. However, neither complained. Red's face was pale and set. "Move briskly," she urged them. "I do not know when he will return."

"He?" Will said, his voice rising in pitch slightly. "Who?"

"Don't ask," Rachel interrupted. "Just walk."

"Briskly" did not describe how they made their way through the forest. Red's leg proved to be a greater hinderance than Rachel had hoped, and she limped along as best she could. It slowed their progress and made Rachel increasingly more nervous, but she couldn't blame the other girl. Not after seeing the damage that had been done to her leg. It was also apparently quite the distance to her home.

They had been walking through the forest for several minutes when a bone-chilling howl split through the silence. Will jumped in surprise, nearly tipping Red over onto the ground. "What the devil was that?" he cried, his voice cracking.

"*Le Loup*," Red said, uttering the words like a curse.

"L-Le what?" Will stammered, staring at her in bemusement.

"The Wolf," Rachel translated quickly, seeing the vexed glare Red turned on the unfortunate outlaw. "How far, Red?"

"Too far!" was Red's panicked response. "Leave me now, and you might make it yourselves. It is not much farther. He smells my blood, he will be upon us soon. Go!"

Both Will and Guy reddened indignantly. "I am *not* abandoning you to some furry monster," Will said flatly. "What do you take me for, an ill-bred swine?"

"Well, you did hold a woman hostage," Guy reminded him.

"With her consent!" Will argued shrilly.

By that time, Rachel was beginning to regret her choice in companions. "STOP FIGHTING!" she yelled at them both. The snuffling, snarling, and howling were getting closer; stealth was no longer any use to them. Oh, why had she brought them with her? Now they were all going to die, and Will and Guy would undergo Final Death. She couldn't shake the memory of the Merry Men's expressions as they bid Will farewell. They would never see him again now. Rachel had little concern for her own welfare. She was the cause of The Story's downfall, and she deserved nothing more than to have her throat torn out by the Big Bad Wolf. But Will and Guy …

87

Rachel's panicked mind was unable to come up with anything even slightly resembling a plan before the Wolf came loping out of the trees. Unlike normal wolves, he strode on his hind legs like a person, over ten feet tall and massively built. Brown, matted and scarred fur covered the length of his body, and beady golden eyes leered down at them. Malevolence seemed to ooze from every inch of him, from the blood-covered claws to the bared fangs. He focused on Red and a look of triumph passed over his face. "Little Red, little Red," he said in a mockingly sing-song voice. "Won't you come and join your granny?"

"*Laisser, Loup!*" Red snapped, but her voice trembled.

"The Wolf can talk," Will said, his eyes wide. "Is that normal?"

Guy ignored Will, stepping in front of Rachel. He drew his sword, the steel sliding against the leather sharply. Unlike Will, he seemed to be taking the talking Wolf in stride. "You'll find us a bit harder to chew than a defenseless girl, beast," he warned.

Red scowled at Guy's back, probably for calling her a defenseless girl. Her reaction was tame compared to the roaring laughter the Wolf let out. "Pardon me while I tremble, Gisborne!" he snorted. "I do not fear you, *traitor*. You should have aligned yourself with the winning side. Now ... now you will be devoured with the rest." Baring his teeth, he approached slowly. As the hulking brute got closer, Guy put his free hand on Rachel's arm, guiding her backwards. Bile rose in her throat, her legs trying to freeze up, but she forced herself to move.

"I have no desire to see the innocent murdered with the guilty," Guy said calmly. His sword never faltered from where it was pointed directly at the Wolf's heart. "The Story will be maintained. I will not allow innocents' lives to be

88

destroyed. I may be considered a 'villain' like you, but we are *nothing* alike." He lunged forward and slashed with his blade.

"Guy!" Rachel cried, her hand falling to her own blade. But she was no fighter! It wasn't like she could do anything aside from distract him. Still, as the blade flashed in the sunlight, reddened with the Wolf's blood, and the claws were raised in the air to smite Guy, she drew the sword and ran forward. She couldn't just let him die.

She acted too late. As she hurtled forward, an arrow from Will flew with her, moving faster and landing in the creature's shoulder. It did little to deter the monster as his claws raked across Guy, sending him flying across the clearing. The blood on the Wolf's chest seemed only to be a surface wound; he turned to Rachel, no indication of his injuries in his maddened eyes. When his gaze lit on Rachel, triumph overcame his expression. "What a prize," he snarled. "The Guardian. You live up to your parents in appearance, at least."

The mention of her parents froze her. She could only stare at him, her hand on the pommel of her still-sheathed blade, trying to comprehend what he was saying. "Andric, look out!" Red yelled just a moment too late. The Wolf took advantage of Rachel's distraction and lunged forward, wrapping his meaty paw around her neck. Rachel gasped as his grip tightened. Her breath was cut off, her throat feeling as if it were collapsing inward; was this what death felt like? It had never occurred to her that she could die, when she had so much more life to live.

Was this how her parents had felt?

After snarling in her face, the Wolf swung her around like a rag doll and slammed her into the ground. His grip on her throat pressed down harder. Out of the corner of her eye, she could see Red's expression of horror, Guy struggling to rise

89

from where he'd been hurled, and Will drawing back another useless arrow to fire at the Wolf. None of them could do anything—none of them *could* do anything. It was just her and the Wolf. Odd, that she had spent most of her life alone, and would likewise die alone. It seemed such a miserable way to go.

When the creature raised his clawed hand above her, preparing to tear out her throat, tears spilled down her cheeks. She would never see her brother again. She wouldn't fix her mistakes. Everything felt like it was happening in slow motion. The Merry Men and all the heroes and good people of The Story would be forced under Final Death by the intruder. She had offered them all false hope and now, they were doomed because of her.

All she could do as she stared up at the claws was pray that it would all be over swiftly.

Chapter 11: The Huntsman

It felt as though the claws were raised above Rachel for forever. She stared up at them, her eyes wide, her breath not coming from the crushing force wrapped around her throat. What would they feel like? Would it hurt, or would she simply lose consciousness before feeling anything?

She never got to find out. In the split second before the claws came down, an arrow sliced through the air and lodged into the Wolf's throat. The monster gave a strangled howl, staggering back, accidentally releasing Rachel. Moving only out of instinct, Rachel scrambled back from him, and Will, who had his bow clutched in his free hand, grabbed her arm, pulling her behind him. Once there, she doubled over, coughing and gagging as air slid down her throat once more.

The Wolf yanked the arrow from his neck, snarling. The blood that dripped slowly down into his fur was a dark red, furthering Rachel's nausea. Yet she couldn't tear her eyes away. "You will pay for that, little boy," the creature snarled at Will.

Will adopted an offended expression. "Oh, come now," he complained. "I'm not *that* young." Although his voice was light, his hand dropped to the quiver at his hip, sliding another arrow free. "Gisborne, any time you want to lend a hand?"

However, Guy was in no condition to be of any assistance. He leaned heavily against the tree he'd been thrown against, panting, blood seeping through his black shirt. "Oh, right," he said sarcastically. He went to draw his sword and growled in pain.

"Leave it!" Red snapped. "You will only get yourself killed." She, too, leaned against a tree, behind Will, her club clutched in her hand.

Guy glared at her, but remained where he was. During the entirety of their conversation, the Wolf had been creeping closer to Will, closing the gap between them. The boy didn't move. He was frozen, the arrow resting on the string of the bow, staring at the massive beast. The Wolf rose to his full height, snarling and foaming at the mouth. Blood still poured from the arrow wound.

"Will, run!" Rachel yelled at him, her voice hoarse. However, the boy remained where he was, pulling the arrow to full draw. She knew why he wouldn't move. If he moved, the Wolf would have a clear line to Red and Rachel. Even if it killed him, he wouldn't let that happen.

"Do not be a fool," Red put in softly.

Will shook his head. "Come get me," he told the Wolf.

The monstrous creature suddenly charged, clearing the distance between them in a split second. Although Will tried to shoot, the arrow slid from the string and he stood before the beast, unarmed, unable to defend himself. Still, he didn't move. "Get out of the way, you imbecile!" Red shouted.

But the young outlaw simply squeezed his eyes shut. His face was an ashen grey and his lips moved in a silent prayer that only he knew. Rachel wished she could tear her eyes away, but she couldn't. Tears fell down her cheeks, not because she knew him well, but because she knew that his death would only be her fault. Even Guy looked stunned and unhappy.

Just as the Wolf raised his paw to tear out Will's throat, the boy lunged forward with a small hunting knife. Although it impaled the creature, the strike made no difference and the Wolf's arm still struck Will, sending him staggering to the ground, obviously dazed. Once more, the claws of death were raised, but there was no hesitation this time. They descended towards the Wolf's victim with brutal efficiency.

A *crack* reached Rachel's ears, and she watched in shock as a crossbow bolt whistled past her head to impale itself into the Wolf's wrist. The pain skewed the Wolf's aim and he missed Will's throat, raking his claws over his chest instead. Blood dripped from the wounds on Will and from the monster's wrist as he swung towards Rachel. Before she could even think to scream, another quarrel flew and dug itself into the Wolf's chest. Whimpering piteously, the creature gave one last half-hearted snarl before loping away.

"*Oncle!*" Red cried, the relief in her voice obvious.

Rachel turned to look, wanting to go to Will but still too weak. Their rescuer, Red's uncle, stood taller than Guy, with ash-streaked blond hair and dark eyes. His face, chiseled and grizzled, was grim as he took in the injured and fearful group. The two small crossbows he held were lowered slowly, both unloaded. "Red. *Ma chère.* Are you well?"

Slowly, Red nodded, sinking into a seated position. "*Oui.* Thanks to you."

He gave a smile that dispelled the saturnine expression on his face and revealed laugh lines etched deeply into his mouth and eyes. "I am always glad to be of service, *Rouge*," he said. However, his gaze traveled past Red to the others, landing on the bleeding Will and Guy. "And your new friends are …?"

"Will Scarlet, Guy of Gisborne, Rachel Andric," Red replied. "They need medical attention."

"Then we shall supply it as best we can," the man said. He reached down to Rachel, and her gaze slid to his leg—or lack thereof. His right leg was wooden from the knee down. She tried to tear her gaze away, but the man had already seen her looking. "It is nothing," he told her. "Do not be ashamed.

Many people look at me in such a way. I do not mind anymore." He took her hand, guiding her to her feet. She didn't protest—her throat felt as if it had been slashed apart, and each breath hurt. The man watched her with some concern for a moment before turning to Guy. "Can you walk?"

Possibly not wanting to be mistaken for being weak, Guy stood up straighter and nodded curtly. "Of course."

After watching him thoughtfully for a moment, the man dismissed him and turned to Will, helping the bleeding outlaw to his feet and sliding an arm under the boy's shoulders. Will looked up at him, blinking almost drowsily. "Th-thank you," he whispered, his gaze sliding down to the blood on his chest. His shirt was torn and shredded.

The man smiled congenially. "Do not thank me yet," he replied. "We have yet to reach my home."

"Who ... who are you?" Rachel said, before breaking off to clear her throat. It just felt *wrong*.

"I am called The Huntsman," he answered, bowing slightly. "Sometimes called Charles, but it makes little difference to me. I prefer my title. Shall we go, Lady Andric?"

She glanced at the others, rubbing the last remnants of her tears from her cheeks. They had survived; Will hadn't had his throat torn out, thanks to The Huntsman. The relief she felt was overwhelming, along with her desire to have somewhere comfortable to sit and rest for a while. "Yes," she said, smiling a tiny bit at the man. "Please."

With that, they set off through the forest, Rachel praying that she would never encounter the Wolf again.

Chapter 12: Former Guardian

The group made their way through the forest without incident. Perhaps the Wolf was still licking his wounds, or he was frightened off by The Huntsman's crossbows. Whatever the case, they reached a small log cabin situated in the middle of the woods. Evidence of the attacks from the Big Bad Wolf were etched into the wood of the abode, gouged into the house by the Wolf's claws. However, none of them seemed to have pierced the sturdy structure.

Leaning on her uncle, Red led the way awkwardly up the stairs. Between her and The Huntsman's injured and missing legs, they were walking on two together. A reluctant Will was leaning on Guy, shooting him suspicious looks and just all around looking uncomfortable. Rachel walked behind them, rubbing her throat. It just ... hurt.

The Huntsman opened the door and took Red inside. Although Will tried to shove Guy away and mount the stairs himself, he almost face-planted and Guy had to grab his arm again, basically dragging him inside. Once Rachel had gone past the door, The Huntsman swung it shut and placed a heavy wooden bolt over it. "Excellent," he said after a moment.

Rachel cast about the room. It seemed to double as a sitting room and a dining room. Red sat at the small circular table, where three other chairs were arranged. A simple chair sat near the wall, possibly belonging to The Huntsman. The whole place smelled of wood and smoke. Rachel guessed it to have about four rooms, though she couldn't see beyond the room they were in. One door must have led to the kitchen.

"Have a seat, Will," The Huntsman said congenially. Guy looked relieved to be free of Will and dumped him into the seat. The redhaired outlaw glared at him but said nothing.

Rachel noticed with some concern that the pallor of his face was swiftly draining of all color.

"Will he be alright?" she asked worriedly.

The Huntsman smiled at her. "Of course," he replied. "I have some herbs to apply to his wounds. They will prevent infection and speed up the healing." He moved surprisingly gracefully through to the kitchen, returning a moment later with two bowls full of water, a few cloths, and bandages over his shoulder. "Lady Andric, would you be so kind as to retrieve the small bowl from beside the fire in the kitchen?"

Rachel nodded, retreating from the room as The Huntsman began removing Red's bloodstained bandages. The scent of blood hung heavy in the air as she returned with the bowl of smashed-up herbs, and she swallowed anxiously. She took to breathing through her mouth, and avoided looking at Red's torn-up ankle as she placed the bowl beside The Huntsman. He looked up with a smile as he cleaned the young woman's wounds. "*Merci*," he said, inclining his head to her.

Rachel nodded before moving towards the door. The Huntsman had evidently dismissed her as he turned his attention back to Red. "Sir Guy, if you would be so kind as to take the other bowl and start cleaning young Will's wounds?"

Guy, from his position in the corner of the room, jumped as if he'd been stung when the man hailed him. "I, ah, I'm not skilled in medicine," he stammered uncomfortably. It was one of the first times Rachel had seen him lose composure.

At the table, Will's eyes slid to the wood top of it, and he looked as comfortable with the arrangement as Guy did. "Perhaps we could just wait for you," he put forward tentatively.

"I think not. The longer those go untended to, the more chance there is for infection. Guy, clean them."
Although on the top of his voice, The Huntsman sounded

congenial and cheerful, there was a hard note beneath it that indicated he did not want to be refused again. Rachel turned her gaze to Guy, whose cheeks had reddened.

"I don't know how." Guy's admission was quiet, and Rachel received a shock. It wasn't that he didn't want to clean the wounds—it was that he didn't know *how* to. He must never have learned the art of medicine as a knight.

Evidently, The Huntsman realized he was telling the truth. "Nonsense!" he said, his voice returning to its normal cheery tone. "Just a bit of cleaning the wound. Rather like dusting, except it's blood and not dust, *oui*? I would ask the Lady Andric to do it, but she seems to be a bit ill ..."

It was Rachel's turn to blush. She didn't appreciate him bringing her phobia of blood to light. "I ... I could do it," she whispered.

Either The Huntsman didn't hear her or he didn't care. His gaze switched from Red's ankle to Guy. "Come now. It is just a little favor while I tend to Red. Surely you can spare the man who saved your lives that much of a courtesy, *oui*?"

The two men stared at each other for a moment before Guy looked at Will. The outlaw stared back, neither looking particularly thrilled with the arrangement. Rachel realized swiftly that The Huntsman was, in a strange way, trying to help her. If they were to succeed against the intruder, she needed her companions to get along. This was the first step towards that.

Finally, Guy nodded reluctantly and picked up both the bowl and the cloths. "Alright," he said. He then instructed Will abruptly to take off his shirt, which the boy did, still staring at him with traces of suspicion in his eyes. Once the shirt had been removed, exposing the ugly red wounds beneath still oozing blood, Guy started scrubbing at them.

Will bit down on his lip hard, probably to keep from making any sounds of pain.

Meanwhile, The Huntsman was applying his poultice to Red's ankle. "You should not have gone out alone," he admonished her softly as he gazed at the bloodied mess of cloths. "Without these people, you would be dead."

"The Wolf should have claimed his last victim, *Oncle*," Red answered in the same vein, looking uncomfortably at their guests. Rachel looked away, trying not to appear too interested in what they were saying. "I wanted to kill him for all the people he has killed."

"With what?" The Huntsman held up her club. "Did you intend to bludgeon him to death? You mean too much for me to let you do such a foolish thing."

Rachel stared at the floor, wishing she could be anywhere but in the cabin with its awkward conversations, open animosity, and the scent of blood hanging heavily over her. She struggled to ignore the puddles of red that had gathered beneath Red's newly-bandaged ankle and Will's gouged chest.

With a great amount of nervousness, she looked up at Will and Guy. Although there was an awkward silence between them, Will's wounds weren't torn open or bleeding everywhere. It seemed to be going rather well, and she breathed a sigh of relief. Even if neither of them were saying anything, it was still an improvement over the arguing they'd been doing before, in the woods.

"Lady Andric," The Huntsman said. She turned to him, surprised. He stood up, grunting slightly. "Ah, these old bones are not intended to kneel down, Red." He patted the young woman's arm before turning back to Rachel. She couldn't help but think that he wasn't as old as he made himself out to be—perhaps his late thirties, but that was as old as she would have pegged him to be. "Would you join me, in the next room?" he requested, indicating the door opposite the one leading to the kitchen.

Rachel shrugged. "Why?" It came out harsher than she'd intended.

"Because, I want to know why The Story is currently being torn to pieces by someone who should not be here," he replied, his tone matching her own icy voice.

The blush that rose to her cheeks hurt. "He got past me and got into The Story," she admitted. The others were carefully avoiding her eyes. She did catch Will watching her, and he swiftly looked away.

"Perhaps we can speak in private?" The Huntsman urged.

Rachel shook her head slightly. "Why can't we speak in front of them?" she asked, indicating her companions. "There's nothing that I don't want them to hear about this."

"Perhaps not about this ... but what of other matters?" The Huntsman's eyebrows were raised.

Other matters? Rachel stared at him for several seconds, feeling as if he'd pulled all the air from her lungs. When she spoke, it was with a significantly icier tone than previously. "I don't know what you're suggesting."

"Your family." Two words were all it took to make all color retreat from Rachel's face. This time, the others couldn't pretend that they weren't curious, and all eyes flicked up to the two speaking.

Rachel took in a deep, slow breath. Maybe her companions would find out at some point, but not now. Not when she hadn't yet had the chance to understand. "Very well," she said, forcing a calm she definitely didn't feel.

The Huntsman gently took her arm and guided her from the room. Even with her back to the others, Rachel could still feel their eyes, practically boring into her back. The room that he took her to was, surprisingly enough, a library, full of shelves with books. Hundreds of them. She leaned her head back slightly, breathing in the smell of leather and the pages, along with the wood. It was no longer oppressive, like that of the blood.

The Huntsman closed the door behind her, breaking her out of her reverie. She turned to him. "What do you know of my family?" she asked immediately. There was no point in beating around the bush with him.

The Huntsman ignored her words, instead turning to face her. "How is Ewan?" he said congenially.

At the mention of her older brother's name, she flinched. "How did you know Ewan?"

The Huntsman's eyebrows shot up at the past tense. "Has something happened to him?" he questioned.

Rachel turned away, putting her head in her hands. "You wouldn't understand. Nobody here would."

"Ah. I see." After regarding her for several seconds, The Huntsman made his way over to one of his bookshelves and pulled out an old, leather-bound copy. It only took him a few seconds of flipping through the pages to find what he was looking for, and he handed the open book to Rachel. "Is that him?" he asked gently.

Her hands trembling, she took the story and turned it to face her. For a brief moment, she squeezed her eyes shut, hardly daring to look. Finally, after telling herself that she had to look or argue with herself for all of eternity, she opened them again and looked down. Written on the top of the page were the words, *"Minor gods of Ancient Greece"*. She traced her finger down the paper, locating a name and several paragraphs written about one of the gods. The picture on the opposite page showed a young man, with tousled black hair and pale skin. The bottom of the picture claimed the name of the young man as "Morpheus, god of sleep and dreams", but Rachel knew better. Her gaze located those familiar, cold, clear-blue eyes, staring up at her. The standard Andric family trait.

She tore her eyes away, and looked up at The Huntsman. "How did you find him?" she asked.

He shrugged innocently. "It was not hard. I have been looking at those eyes for five years, Rachel. At least give me the credit to recognize the familiar trait of the Andric eyes. I knew your parents, and I met him when he was young, a new Guardian. Always such a rebel, just like his father."

Rachel shifted uncomfortably. "I wish he hadn't been such a rebel," she admitted softly. "But ... how much do you know?" As much as she was desperate to ask him about her parents, she knew that now was not the time. Duty as a sister was pulling at her to ask about Ewan.

The Huntsman sat down on the only wooden chair in the room, his face haggard. "I know because ... he is like me."

It was as if he'd pulled a blindfold from off her eyes. "You're a Guardian," she said.

The expression on his face became a bitter smile. "More appropriately, I *was* a Guardian," he replied. "The first to be written into The Story for breaking the rules."

She stared at him. Everyone knew about the first Guardian who had broken the rules. It was basically a legend among all of them. He had ventured into the Cinderella Story to fix a mistake and accidentally switched the golden slippers for glass ones. In keeping with the rules of the Guardians to maintain The Story, the offender had been written into The Story and set a precedent. Nobody had ever known the identity of the man written in. "I'm sorry," she whispered, unable to meet his eyes.

His laugh was soft. "Do not apologize to me," he told her, reaching forward and patting her arm. "At least I am a hero in my Story, *oui*? It would have not been very exciting for me if they had put me into Cinderella's Story, now would it have been? At least here, I have Red," he added, a touch more seriously.

"I guess you're right." She wondered if Ewan had anyone with him. "I just never understood why the Guardians don't just fix the mistakes, *especially* if they're just mistakes, and leave the offender alone. I mean, you didn't mean to switch the slippers, right?"

With no warning, The Huntsman's dour expression was brightened by an impish grin. "Accidentally?" he repeated. "Well, that part of the Guardians' legend might have been, ah, adjusted. All I told the Fairy Godmother was that glass would look *much* better than gold. Don't you think?" He adopted an innocent face. "That is accidental, is it not?"

Rachel just stared at him, unable to decide if he was joking or not. She never could tell. "Ewan. He—his wasn't accidental. Not at all."

He cocked his head, silently inviting her to elaborate further. She didn't know why she did. Perhaps there was just something trustworthy about him, or she just needed to get it off her chest. Whatever the case, she continued speaking. "He hated the fact that certain people had to die over and over in The Story, so one day ... one stupid, ridiculous day ... he decided to save the life of someone in The Story."

"Ah." The Huntsman was once again utterly serious.

Somewhere, somehow, Rachel found the strength to carry on. "He went into the Trojan War Story," she said. She just needed to tell it to *someone*. "He stopped Paris from shooting Achilles. The Guardians, they went in ... they killed

102

him. Achilles. Then they dealt with Ewan. He was standing in front of me, boasting about what he'd done, and then the next second he was just—gone." Bitterly, she snapped her fingers together. "Not a word about what Story he'd been sent to. Nothing. Just ... taken."

The Huntsman inclined his head slightly, sighing. "I know loss. As does Red," he added, jerking his head towards the dining room. "I cannot tell you the joy it gives me, to be able to enlighten you as to your brother's location."

The words made Rachel bite down on her lip, hard. "But should I pursue it?" she asked. "Or am I just going to torment myself with what could've been?"

"Rachel, if you want an old cripple's opinion, you should never let a chance to see a member of your family that you thought lost go by," he told her. "And if I am being honest, you may not have much time left to see him before he looks at you and doesn't know who you are."

"You mean ... you mean, he'll forget?" Rachel asked, aghast. "But how could he forget me? I'm his sister!"

"I am not saying that he already has," The Huntsman assured her. "But I must warn you that I myself retain no memories of my previous life, other than the simple fact that I was a Guardian. Do you really want him to look at you in such a way?"

A cold hand clutched at Rachel's heart, increased by the ominous way in which The Huntsman was speaking. "How could he forget me?" she whispered, staring down at her feet. What would she do if he already *had* forgotten her? Should she really expose herself to that sort of terrible pain?

The Huntsman squeezed her arm gently. "Take a chance, Rachel," he urged her. "Do not let the moment pass you if you have the chance. Now, come," he added, rising and dismissing the subject for the time being. "Let us see how Will and Sir Guy are getting along, shall we?"

Chapter 13: A Quiet Night

Much to Rachel's surprise, Guy had tended to Will's wound well, and even finished wrapping Red's ankle for her. The young French woman was seated by the now-lit fireplace, was sewing Will's shirt where it had been savaged by the claws. Someone had made the attempt to clean the blood from it, and it now just looked vaguely dirty. When Rachel and The Huntsman returned to the main room, all three of its occupants turned and looked at them. Rachel felt her cheeks turn a bright red.

However, The Huntsman gave them no time to stare. He took hold of Rachel's arm and steered her towards the kitchen. "If you are going to remain here for the night, we should prepare a meal, do you think?" he said cheerily. To the others, he added, "Guy, you are welcome to join us. Will, just remain where you are. I do not think you want to reopen those wounds, *oui*?"

Will looked relieved that he hadn't been called upon to stand up. "Yes, sir," he said dutifully, and settled back into the chair. "How long do you think it will take them to mend?"

"There will be scarring, I believe," The Huntsman said thoughtfully. "However, you should be well enough to move around in a day or so. Calendula will do you good and prevent infection."

"Do I have to eat it?" Will asked, his face scrunching up in displeasure.

The Huntsman laughed, a booming sound that caused everyone in the room to jump. "*Oncle*, must you?" Red rebuked him in an annoyed way.

He patted her shoulder as he walked past. "Ahh, it is always good to laugh, *ma chère*," he told her. "What is life without laughter? Dull. And no, Will, you do not have to eat calendula. It is in the poultice that is on your wounds."

"Oh." Will's cheeks turned as red as his hair. "Right. Well, umm, thank you."

"*De rien*," The Huntsman replied. He pulled Rachel along with him into the kitchen, and Guy followed like a silent shadow.

As the door to the kitchen swung closed behind them, Rachel heard Will ask Red, "What does that mean?" She struggled to stifle her laughter as Red translated for the outlaw. He was hopelessly out of his depth.

. . . . .

Dinner was comprised of a flavorful soup with chunks of venison and pheasant in it. Rachel did very little in helping to prepare for it, mostly watching The Huntsman do everything. The ease with which he moved around, even with his absence of a leg, was astonishing. The kitchen was small, a massive fireplace taking up most of the space. As a result, Guy and Rachel basically stood in the corner and observed the cook at work.

It took about two hours to cook. After the first hour, The Huntsman sent them both back out with Will and Red. The former looked utterly bored, since Red was curled up in her chair and reading a book. He started talking nonstop to Rachel about nonsense while Guy sighed at his behavior. However, the next hour until dinner was prepared was more pleasant to Rachel than any time she'd spent before. There was no impending doom, no worried outlaws sending one of their own into danger, and just a generally cheerful atmosphere. Plus, Will really didn't require much of a response when conversing.

106

The dinner tasted as good as it smelled. When The Huntsman rejoined them, he and Will talked the most, providing most of the conversation at the table. It gave Rachel a chance to think about what The Huntsman had shown her in the library, since he was mostly asking Will and Guy about their Story. Would Ewan even recognize her? How could she bear it if he looked at her with his eyes that were so like their father's, and not know who she was? For years, she'd dared to dream that she would meet him again. Now, she didn't know if she wanted to. Fear and guilt ate away at her, slowly dissolving the good atmosphere around her. The others seemed unaware of her brooding, though more than once, she caught Red's grey eyes watching her intently.

Dinner ended and the group disbanded. The Huntsman showed Guy and Will to their shared room, which was most likely The Huntsman's. He put a pallet on the floor of the kitchen for himself to sleep on, while Rachel was allowed to sleep in the library when she asked. Red remained in the dining room area.

Rachel now sat in one of the chairs in the library, the Greek myths book open on her lap. Ewan stared up at her, his mouth twitching up in a smile, his bangs falling slightly into his eyes. Slowly, she drew her finger over his face, remembering his teasing, their arguments, and the long nights they'd spent together after their parents' death. Curled in front of the fireplace, listening to one of the storms that was common to their little island. No words would pass between them. They would just sit there together ... remembering.

Without warning, tears spilled down her cheeks, falling onto the page. Swiftly, she closed the book to keep it from getting damaged and covered her face. She wasn't ready for this, for *any* of this. She wanted him by her side, helping her. She needed someone to help her on, convince her she was doing the right thing. If anyone underwent Final Death, there could be no one to blame but herself. The intruder had escaped into The Story on her watch, and it was up to her to fix it. That weight on her shoulders was more than she'd ever wanted. She *needed* Ewan's comforting presence, his teasing, the way he'd tug at one of her blonde curls when she got sad. But what if all the things she was remembering, he didn't?

Rachel sniffed, trying to regain some form of control over her raging emotions. It had been a long time since she'd let herself cry like that, and she found that she didn't enjoy it one bit. It hurt too much to let herself feel like this. She leaned her head back in the chair, wishing she could fall asleep and make it all go away.

"Are you well?" The unexpected voice was accompanied by the sound of the door closing. Rachel lifted her head to see Red Riding Hood standing just in the doorframe, looking odd without her red cloak. Her white nightgown drifted down to the floor, her feet bare aside from the bandages wrapped around her left leg.

Rachel rubbed at her cheeks, trying to hide the tracks of tears there. "Oh ... well enough," she said after an awkward moment of silence passed between them. "What—what are you doing here?"

Red shrugged. "I thought I heard something. So I came to see if you were alright. And you are."

"So I am." For a moment, the two young women regarded each other. Red looked about as comfortable with the current situation as Rachel felt, and she wasn't sure why Red was still there—or even why she'd come at all.

"I am glad you are well," Red put forward after a long moment. "I suppose you are going to tell me that you were crying for no reason?"

Rachel shrugged slightly. "It's nothing important. Nothing you need to worry about, anyway."

A cold look passed over Red's face. "Indeed." She looked almost as if she were planning on leaving, but by the light of the candle beside Rachel, her gaze fell on the book of Greek myths. "Why do you have that?" There was an oddly defensive tone to Red's voice that made Rachel answer truthfully.

"It ... one of the pages in here. Morpheus. I know him."

Red narrowed her eyes slightly before relaxing her tense stance. "It is your brother, is it not? Ewan."

Rachel pursed her lips. "Yes. It's Ewan. But how do you ...?"

"I met him, once. When I was a child. He came when I lost my basket to bring to my grandmother." Red's voice was little more than a whisper. "He was very kind to me."

Rachel shook her head miserably. "He wasn't being kind. He was making sure The Story went the way it was supposed to. Without your basket, you wouldn't have gone to your grandmother's house and you wouldn't have been swallowed whole by the Wolf."

"I am aware of that," Red answered calmly. "However, he was very good to me. And there was a certain reluctance to him. It was as if he did not want to do it, but knew that he had to. I do not regret meeting your brother."

That response made Rachel bite down hard on her lower lip. "Neither do I," she said, her voice breaking, and she covered her face again. "But ... but what if he doesn't ..."

Red hesitated, looking almost like she wanted to leave. However, she moved towards Rachel and sat down in the chair next to Rachel's. "What if he doesn't—what?" she pressed gently.

"The Huntsman said he might not remember me," Rachel answered, trying to gulp down her tears. "I couldn't stand it if that turned out to be true."

"You will not know unless you go, *oui*?" Red retorted, her voice quiet. "Is it worse to look upon your loved one and have them not recognize you, or to never see them again at all?"

Rachel sighed. "I'd already resigned myself to the fact that I was never going to see him again," she said. "Why expose myself to more pain?"

The French girl shrugged, her raven hair sliding over her shoulder. "Because for family, it is worth it, is it not?" she said. "I would give anything to see my family again. I believe that it is selfish of you not to want that."

"Selfish?" Rachel repeated, a note of disbelief ringing in her voice.

"*Oui.* You are taking from your brother the chance to see his sister again because you are too afraid." Red stood up, her voice hard as a rock. "Perhaps you never thought about it that way. Instead of thinking that he *won't* remember you, consider that he still might."

"True …" Rachel hadn't really thought about it like that. However, she didn't want to. That would be offering too much hope into her mind, when she worried that raising her hopes would only result in them being dashed to the ground and shattered like glass. "But, still."

"There is no 'but, still'," Red answered flatly. "There is just what you are willing to do, and what you are not willing to do. There is nothing in between. Do you think that people who have lost their families do not wish for every moment of their lives that they could see them again? Even if it is to just see them? What does it matter if he does not remember you? You remember him, do you not? Should that not be enough for you?"

Rachel looked away, trying not to meet Red's eye. "What happened to your family?"

"Dead," Red replied with a savage tone. "Killed by the Wolf, after Uncle Charles's attempt to drown him failed. It was not supposed to be like that, I know. But it happened. Uncle Charles returned me to my home village, with my parents and my *grand-mère* alongside me. I was home once more. I had no fear, I could *live* as a normal girl, for the first time in my life. And for a few years, I did. Until the Wolf returned. He destroyed my entire village, clawed my leg to prevent me from running ... and murdered them all in front of me. My parents, my ... my grandmother, even my older brother. Just as he was about to kill me, *Oncle* came and shot him, frightening him away. He is the only one that the Wolf fears. And because of that, Uncle Charles did not wish me to live with him. He brought me to a town and tried to get the people to keep me there. Although they agreed, once he had departed, they treated me as a blight upon them. A *malédiction* upon them. To them, I was worse than worthless."

After a moment's pause, Red tugged her gown away from her shoulder, revealing the scar of a welt there. "A woman threw a rock at me and gave me that scar. It became apparent to me that to stay would be to die. They despised me so greatly that I would be killed soon if I was not careful. So, I ran. I ran to my *oncle*, and he finally decided to take me into his home. And that is why I am here."

"I don't understand," Rachel said. "Your Story should've ended when you were cut from the belly of the Wolf. Why didn't it?"

"How should I know?" Red replied with a shrug. "The fact remains that it did not. And as a result, my family perished. I would give my life to see them again, one final time, as you have been given the chance to do. So forgive me for thinking you selfish for not accepting this beautiful, wonderful chance."

Without any warning, Red stood up and walked out of the library, leaving Rachel alone to her thoughts.

.   .   .   .   .

It hadn't taken much to get Will to take the only bed in his shared room with Gisborne. The knight had gruffly told Will that, because he was wounded, he should sleep on the bed, and Will hadn't protested at all. Now he lay under the covers, astonished at how *comfortable* a bed was after years of sleeping on the hard ground of Sherwood Forest.

There was the rustling of fabric and a hard *thud* from the floor. Then Gisborne spoke. "Scarlet ... are you still awake?"

Will rolled over to face him. Pain seemed to lace through his whole body when his scratches rubbed against their bandages. "Yes. What is it?"

The knight was rubbing his shoulder, where he'd evidently smacked it against the wooden floor. "I've been thinking. Lady Rachel is extremely out of her depth. She doesn't belong in our world, she knows little of our ways, and yet she is willing to risk her life to save us and our world."

"Yes ...?" Will wasn't really sure where Gisborne was trying to go with this.

There was a long moment of silence between them. At first, Will just assumed that Guy had fallen asleep again and prepared to do the same thing himself. The deep voice of his sort-of companion broke through the fog of sleep. "Perhaps we should begin to try and accept each other's presence," Guy said. "After all, this quest will likely take some time. And we *are* supposed to be allies."

Will rolled onto his back and stared at the ceiling. "But I don't like you much," he said. That was a severe understatement. He despised Gisborne. The man had stood by and watched as The Sheriff had killed Will's mother, Rowena, in front of him. And yet, he knew Gisborne had a point. If they were to succeed, they needed to work together.

"I'm not asking you to like me," Gisborne answered flatly. "I despise you."

"Ouch," Will said.

Gisborne sighed audibly. "Be serious, Scarlet. What I'm suggesting is that we try and curb our arguments a bit, for her sake more than our own. After all, we're not going to get anywhere if we're always at each other's throats, are we?"

"True." Will considered Gisborne's suggestion. It wasn't impossible, to be honest. Although he disliked the man, he liked Rachel, and wanted to impress her. Even if that meant losing himself the chance to earn some points insulting Gisborne. He sighed before rolling to the side of the bed and extending his hand down, towards Gisborne, fingers straight. "Truce?" he asked.

Gisborne considered him for a moment before shaking his hand. "Truce," he agreed. "By the way ... I never knew that you knew so much about medicine."

"Impressed?" Will asked with amusement.

"Let's just say it was unexpected," Gisborne answered.

"Well, I guess I'll always be keeping you on your toes," Will said, chuckling as he rolled over and closed his eyes.

He was asleep in moments.

Chapter 14: Breakfast

The following morning, Rachel woke feeling dazed, struggling to remember where she was. It was still dark, and she didn't know why until a distant rumble of thunder broke through her fog. It was pouring outside, slapping the ground with the gentle noise only rain could make.

Rachel hadn't even left her chair. At some point after her conversation with Red, she must have fallen asleep in it. Her blonde hair was matted to her cheek, and her head felt heavy. However, as she rose and smoothed out her blouse, she felt a little better about herself. At least she looked presentable.

Someone knocked on the door, and the young woman looked up. "Yes?" she said, tugging her fingers through her snarled hair.

The door opened, and Guy looked in, his hand on the knob. "The Huntsman says that it is breakfast," he said, looking vaguely awkward.

Rachel smiled a little at him. "Thanks, Guy. I'll be out in a minute."

The knight gave a small and rather curt nod before hastily retreating. Chuckling over his embarrassment, Rachel finished combing through her hair with her fingers and went out into the dining room. Will was sitting at the table already, eating some bacon. He looked up when Rachel came in. "Good morning," he said. "Sleep well?"

"Well enough." Rachel sat down beside him. "Where'd you get the bacon?"

"From The Huntsman," he explained. "I suppose he gets them from a nearby village."

"Seems like a lot of danger for a few pieces of pork," Rachel muttered, grabbing a few pieces from the plate in the middle of the table. It was uncannily good bacon, though she supposed a huntsman would know the best way to flavor and cook the meat.

Will shrugged, crunching down on a piece of his own. "I don't know about danger, but I'd risk my life for this, it's that good," he said. "Seen the others yet?"

"Guy told me it was time to eat. Haven't seen anyone else," Rachel said, privately hoping she *wouldn't* see Red after their awkward conversation from the previous night. The words spoken between them still hung heavy in her mind.

Will shrugged congenially. "Well, I suppose we'll have to be good enough company for the both of us," he commented. He leaned back in his chair. "That talking wolf yesterday ... is it often you come across something that frightening in The Story?"

Rachel shrugged. "I don't really know," she admitted. "This is my first time here. But I've read things. Dragons, lions, stuff like that. The Wolf was just ... just a little too creepy for my tastes."

Will chuckled slightly. "Mine too. Hopefully, that's the last we've seen of him."

"Hopefully," Rachel agreed, crunching on more bacon. "I've had enough of that creature to last me for a lifetime."

They laughed together quietly, wondering where the others had gone. Without warning, Guy came in from outside and sat down at the table, taking a piece of bacon. Although he didn't say anything, his dark eyes scanned the other two a few times before sliding down to the table. Will spoke when it became apparent that Guy wouldn't. "What were you up to?" he asked cheerily.

"None of your business." Guy cast him a glare before returning to his bacon.

Rachel tapped her fingers against the wooden table. "It *is* my business, though, since I invited you along on this quest," she pointed out.

Although he crinkled his nose in displeasure, he did respond, which was a plus in Rachel's eyes. "I was cutting wood for The Huntsman while he made breakfast," he said. "Red came out with me."

"Red?" Will frowned. "Why'd she go out with you?"

"How should I know?" Guy bit back angrily. "Is she not her own person? Perhaps she just wanted a breath of fresh air."

But there was an undertone in Guy's voice that made Rachel seriously doubt that was true. She narrowed her eyes at Guy, who saw her expression and swiftly looked away. So ... she'd told him about Ewan, probably. Which made Will the only one who *didn't* know. He was blissfully ignorant, crunching on bacon and even humming something. What sort of a maniac was he?

They continued eating in silence. The amount of bacon on the table was astonishing—there had to be more than fifty pieces, and Will had been eating for about ten minutes already. Rachel ate five or six before feeling too full to eat anymore, and Will ... was still eating.

Red and The Huntsman emerged from the kitchen, the latter looking displeased about something. Red had a stubborn expression on her face as she limped to a chair and sat down. Even Will couldn't ignore the discomfort of *that* situation, and he stopped eating to look at the uncle and niece. "Something wrong?" he asked.

"It is nothing," The Huntsman said, shooting Red a glare. It was so peculiar from his behavior the previous day that all three of his guests just stared at him blankly. Catching their stares, he grimaced and grabbed a piece of bacon. "It is family matters. A foolish attempt to do something that will only result in trouble."

Red crossed her arms and looked away, not even meeting anyone's eyes. She looked for all the world like a sulking child. "A foolish attempt, perhaps. But it was for you that I was going to do it."

"Be that as it may, heroic sacrifices will still only end up with one thing. You, dead." The Huntsman frowned, his displeasure at the turn of events evident. "Do not force me to go through that grief, Red."

"And you expect me to want you to perish at the Wolf's hands?" Red exclaimed indignantly. "Why do you not understand that? However much you care about me, I care about you just as much. Perhaps more."

"I understand that," The Huntsman said, obviously trying for a calmer tone of voice. "But killing yourself will get you nowhere. Do you want me to lose the only family I have left? When we face the Wolf, we shall do it together."

Red looked away, unable to protest that. The others looked down at the table, trying to avoid their gazes. It had been a family discussion, and none of them wanted to get involved. Perhaps sensing their displeasure in the situation, The Huntsman forced a smile. "My apologies. I am making you all uncomfortable."

"Oh, no, of course not," Rachel said. But the tone of voice she used probably revealed her own discomfort.

Will was scratching at his chest. "Umm ... you are," he said.

The Huntsman guffawed. "Thank you for your honesty!" he replied, and his laughter lightened the mood considerably. Even Red looked as if she was trying not to smile. "Did you enjoy the bacon I made?"

"It was good," Guy said gruffly. However, his attention was fixed less on the bacon and more on Rachel. "What is the plan for today?" he added.

Rachel shrugged. "I don't know. We came here for a purpose, but I haven't figured out what sort of a hand the intruder had in this Story. Until I do, we can't leave. I don't want to leave anyone in any sort of peril. Also ..."

They all looked at her, the only sound being a loud *crunch* from Will as he bit down on yet another piece of bacon. She blushed and tried to hide it. "It's just that, yesterday, I felt like someone was following me. And it wasn't the Wolf. I saw black clothes."

The Huntsman sat back in his chair, frowning. "Hmm ... if the Wolf was not attacking this black-clothed individual, then I believe we can assume them to be in ... how do you say ... cohesiveness?"

"Cahoots," Rachel said, unable to think of any other word to use. "Which means we need to figure out who it is, and why the intruder's sent him or her here."

Will swallowed. "Back out with the creepy talking wolf?" he said a trifle anxiously.

"Not yet," Rachel said. "If the intruder sent his minion here to bother us, then I'd be willing to bet that he or she will approach us before long. And if they don't, then we go to meet them by luring them here. Not far enough from the house that we'll get cut off before we can barricade ourselves in again, but not close enough that they'll know what we're doing."

"It is a solid plan," Red agreed, somewhat reluctantly. Unlike the others, she had not yet touched the breakfast. "Unless, of course, they realize what you are attempting."

"We shall see," Guy said.

Will was still rubbing at his chest. Rachel narrowed her eyes at him, noting his ghastly-white pallor and the idle way he scratched. "Will," she said. "Are you alright?"

The boy looked up guiltily. "Oh yes. Of course I am!" he answered brightly—too brightly, in her opinion. Something was not quite right with him.

The Huntsman stood, limping over to Will. "Oh, *mon cher*, you are a terrible liar," he told him, pulling his chair out to give him more room.

"Did he just call him 'my dear'?" Guy muttered with a frown.

"My dear *boy*," Rachel corrected him. "It's a term of endearment."

"Not sure what's so endearing about a foolish outlaw who refuses to admit when he's injured," Guy said, still under his breath.

Both Rachel and Red glared at him. He shrugged innocently, tracing the imperfections in the wood with his fingertip. Meanwhile, The Huntsman was removing Will's shirt gently, though the movement still made the boy wince in pain. "Easy," The Huntsman whispered to him. "Easy. Just concentrate on something other than the pain, hm?"

"Oh, easy for you to say," Will said, grimacing again. "You're not the one who has to deal with it. I thought that calendula paste-stuff was supposed to help."

"It was," The Huntsman answered, using a knife to expertly slice through the bandages around Will's torso. "But nothing is infallible, hm? Let me see."

Rachel had to look away as Will's scratched and still-weeping torso was exposed from beneath the bandages. There was pus mixed with the blood, and numerous red marks spiraling out from the original wounds as well. The Huntsman made an annoyed sound in the back of his throat. "Infected," he said.

"But you said—"

"I underestimated two things," The Huntsman said. "Apparently, this new player that your intruder has summoned has made things slightly difficult, *oui*? His wounds are magically infected, hastening the effect. And I am out of calendula."

"It didn't work too well in the first place," Guy said.

The Huntsman sighed. "No, but I can try again. Unless you are a sorcerer who can counter this magic?"

For the first time, Guy flushed and looked away. "No."

"*Bien*," The Huntsman said, looking satisfied. "Then keep your sarcastic comments to yourself, *oui*?"

"But if you're out of calendula, then won't the infection get worse?" Rachel asked worriedly.

"Well ... yes." The man stared down at the table irritably. "Which means we need more."

"And where do you plan on getting more?" Red inquired innocently.

If Rachel had been Red, she wouldn't have added anything to the conversation. The Huntsman glared at her, but she wasn't swayed and simply raised her eyebrows in an inquiring manner. "Someone will have to go out into the forest and get some. It grows in certain areas," he said.

"Go out?" Will said. "With the creepy talking wolf? You're mad. I'm not worth that."

"Do not be modest, William," The Huntsman admonished him. "I would do this for everyone, not just you. Does that make you feel better?"

"Oh ... I suppose," Will answered, shifting slightly uncomfortably in his seat. A thin layer of sweat was visible on his bare chest.

"*Bien.*" The man stood up, glancing at Rachel. "Will you go for me? I am not as fast as I used to be. If the Wolf does approach, then I will not be able to flee from him. We must act quickly. Will has a matter of hours, because of the magic aspect of his injuries. I fear that, if we do not act now, he will die."

"Then I'll go," Rachel said. "Don't worry." She stood up, grabbing her sheathed sword where she'd left it by the corner and belting it around her waist. "Do you just need the calendula?"

"Well," The Huntsman said. "I have a secret recipe for a poultice that contains rosemary and thyme as well—and those herbs also flavor soups in a superb fashion."

Rachel stared at him blankly. "You want me to risk my life for flavoring for soup?" she asked.

The Huntsman smiled innocently. "It is for the poultice," he said.

Will snorted in laughter. "I like soup," he added.

The Huntsman patted his shoulder cheerily. "Guy," he said, growing more serious, "you will go with the Lady Rachel. Two is safer than one, hm? And you two are the only uninjured members of the party."

Rachel opened her mouth to protest too late. "Very well," Guy replied, nodding. Unlike Rachel, he didn't need to retrieve his weapon. The sword was already sitting at his hip when he stood.

She shot The Huntsman a glare, and he purposely ignored her. "Then you had better hurry," he urged them. "The infection will spread quickly. We do not have much time."

121

"You might want a cloak," Red put in, looking irritated at being left out. "It is cold in the morning."

"Right," Rachel agreed, closing her eyes. Although time was of the essence, she figured now would be as good a time as any to try out the Guardian ability to change clothes. It gave her a peculiar tingling sensation in the pit of her stomach, but when she opened her eyes, she had a cloak. There was just one problem ...

"It looks like Red's!" Will exclaimed, delighted.

"Sorry," Rachel said, blushing furiously. "It must've just been on my mind."

"Well, they do say imitation is the greatest form of flattery," Will said. "Or something like that. It suits you."

Now she was blushing for a different reason, and quickly looked away. "Are you ready?" she said to Guy, hoping to change the subject.

Guy arched his eyebrows in a vaguely amused way. "To risk life and limb for soup?" he replied. "Certainly. After you."

Chapter 15: Will's Story

Immediately following Guy's flippant remark, Guy and Rachel left the house in search of the herbs. The Huntsman retired from the dining room and went into the kitchen, where much banging and noise could be heard. Red leaned her elbows on the table, grey eyes fixed on Will. "You've caused a lot of trouble," she commented innocently to him.

Will sighed, rubbing the sweat from his forehead. The whole situation was just very uncomfortable for him. "Seems that I have," he agreed. "Unintentionally, but it doesn't seem to matter."

Red continued to watch him, which was beginning to make him just a little uncomfortable. "Something the matter?" he asked after a long moment.

"Are you truly so blind to everything that has been going on?" she said at last. "You act like nothing is wrong, like no Stories are threatened. As if you do not care. It makes me wonder what sort of a person you are, that you can ignore the suffering and misery going on around you."

"I'm not ignoring it," Will said flatly. He wanted to stand, but his upper torso was in too much pain to allow that. "And I'm not an evil person. It's just ... I have a hard time seeing the whole thing. You know, how bad it *actually* is. I understand the threat to the Merry Men, to my family, and I know it's affected you, but ... beyond that ... The Story just boggles my mind. I know next to nothing about it, and it just doesn't really affect me."

Red frowned. "Everyone understands the concept of The Story."

Will's cheeks flamed. "Oh, don't get all high and mighty," he snapped. "I don't understand it. I must be an idiot, but I don't understand any of it. Not Final Death, not the tales, nothing. And I certainly don't understand how people can say we've lived multiple lives and died numerous times."

That got Red's attention. She stared at him, this time not in a judgmental way, but in a purely shocked way. "You remember … nothing?" she repeated uncertainly.

Still incensed, Will didn't notice the change in her tone. "No, I don't remember anything! That must be another strike against me, isn't it? Not only have I caused a lot of trouble and am a cruel and heartless human being, as well as being an idiot who doesn't understand certain things, I'm also a fool who can't remember anything but this life!"

Red rolled her eyes to heaven. "For heaven's sake, will you listen to me?" she said sharply. Will made a face but fell silent. "I am not insulting your intelligence or your goodness. What I am trying to say is this. You have been in the presence of many conversations concerning The Story, and yet you remember nothing of it. I remember every life I've lived, every time I've been devoured by the Wolf, and every moment that my Story was restarted, since hearing of its existence from Uncle Charles. Yet … you sit here before me, not remembering *anything*. How is that possible?"

Now Will felt *very* uncomfortable. He looked down at the table as if he could bore a hole through it and started tracing the small imperfections and cracks in the wood with the tip of his finger. "How should I know?" he answered, still defensive.

Red put her forearms on the table and banged her forehead on them several times. "For the last time, I am not insulting you!" she cried. "Get this through your thick skull, William Scarlet. You are different! *Comprendre?*"

124

The rapid-fire speech made Will stare at her, and she flushed but didn't break eye contact with him. The words could only allow him to stammer out a few words. "B-but why am I different?"

Red shrugged. "That is what I want to know," she commented. "But it does not seem as if you have the answer to it. Unfortunately."

Will leaned back, rubbing at his chest. Red moved closer to him and slapped his hand. "Do not scratch at it. You will only make it worse," she told him.

"How can I make it worse?" he asked glumly. "I've been magically poisoned and The Huntsman's sent Rachel and Gisborne out to look for soup herbs."

"Don't be so pessimistic," Red rebuked him. "Are you not supposed to be the overly-cheerful one?"

Will shrugged. "This is my second near-death experience in two days," he said heavily. "I'm beginning to think I'm useless."

Red heaved an audible sigh. "Come with me." Before he could protest, she grabbed his arm and dragged him along behind her. It sent spasms of pain up his body, but he was kind of glad that they were doing something other than talking. Conversations with Red were just awkward.

She pulled him into the library and sat him down on the chair. Once he was comfortably seated, the young woman went to the shelves and started searching through them. He could only watch in bemusement as she muttered to herself in French, searching, scanning the shelves. "What *are* you looking for?" he asked after several minutes passed.

"Hush," she told him. "I will let you know."

Will heaved a sigh. "Can't you just let me know now?"

To that, she gave no answer, which he supposed was an answer in of itself. He leaned back in the chair, scooting around to make himself more comfortable. The wood pressed into his bare back, and idly he hoped he wouldn't get any splinters from it. The thought nearly made him laugh, and he disguised the noise by coughing. Red shot him a glance before returning to her search.

Finally, after what felt like forever, she found what she was looking for and pulled a book from the shelf. She muttered something in French before handing the leather-bound copy to Will. "Read it."

"Why?" Will's words came off as sharper than he'd intended.

Red rolled her eyes. "Because I want to show you The Story," she said. "We have time while we wait for the others to come back with your medicine."

Will swallowed anxiously. "I ... I can't."

"What? Why not?" Now Red was staring at him in bemusement.

The outlaw put his head in his hands. "I can't read."

The French girl looked at him for several seconds before flushing slightly. "*Je suis désolé*," she said awkwardly. "You can still open it. There are pictures."

Although Will had no idea what she'd said in French, he still did as he was told and opened the book. Sure enough, the very first pages had pictures, and Will stared at it as if he could bore a hole through the pages. "That's my mum," he whispered. "My adopted mother."

"Adopted?" Red said. "She is not your true mother?"

"She was as true a mother as I ever needed," Will answered, glancing up at her briefly. His mother, Rowena, could have passed for his "true" mother, with her red curly hair sweeping down her back. The only differences were her dark green eyes, laughing as she watched an eight-year-old

Will practice with a little bow he'd made. "Heavens, it looks just like her."

"Of course it does," Red told him. "It is magic. Every book in here is a representation of The Story. That is your Story."

"Every book in here is a Story?" Will raised his eyes from the pages and looked at the hundreds of books in the shelves. "My word ..."

"These are all the people that are being threatened by the intruder's presence," Red said. "I am trying to help you see the ... how do you say ... bigger picture."

Will didn't answer. He was flipping through the Merry Men book again, ignoring the page—or trying to ignore it, at least—where he saw his mother being held by The Sheriff, a sword pointed at her back. Instead, he focused on the pages showing the good times he'd had with the Merry Men. He smiled when he saw that most of the pictures showed Alan playing his lute, no matter what was going on around him. It was uncannily accurate.

It was when he reached the last pages of the book that he paused. "What's this?" he asked Red, holding the book up to her.

The picture was showing Will, older by an indeterminate number of years, his sword unsheathed, his back to a tree. He was surrounded by men. Judging by their black surcoats, they were likely to be The Sheriff's.

Red's eyebrows shot up. "That is your death," she said matter-of-factly. "Not your Final Death, of course, but the one you die every Story cycle."

"I—I *die*?" Will felt like a fish out of water as the words were torn from him in surprise. "But I'm not dead. You can tell, just look at me!"

"You do not understand," Red answered with a sigh. "When you 'die' in The Story, you don't die. It is simply a temporary thing until The Story is restarted. As long as you die according to The Story, then there is nothing to fear."

"You say 'die' in a sentence and expect me not to fear?" Will said, horror-struck. "How can you treat this like it's so ... so ... *normal*?"

Red sighed, limping over to his chair and leaning against it. "It is normal," she told him. "What is not normal is you. If you do not mind my bluntness."

"I *do* mind your bluntness," Will said. "Because you're telling me I'm a freak, for lack of a better term. I'm not abnormal, Red. Maybe you should consider that all *this* is abnormal."

"*Pardon*." The voice from the door made both of them turn quickly to stare. The Huntsman stood there, leaning against the doorframe, watching them. "But, Will ... Red is right. You are different. Not in a bad way, but an interesting way. In all my years as both a Guardian and a member of The Story, I have never met a soul who does not remember their Story when it is spoken of in their presence."

Will slumped back against his seat. "I'm a freak," he said dully.

The Huntsman thumped his way over with his wooden leg to pat Will's shoulder. "Do not think so harshly of yourself," he rebuked him gently. "Just because you are different does not make you a freak, hm? And we shall discover why you are different some time. In the meantime, let us focus on saving your life, *oui*?"

Will looked at him and nodded. "A-alright." He sought a way to change the subject. "Sir, what was Rachel talking to you about?"

"Ah," The Huntsman said. "We were discussing the fate of her brother, Ewan. It would most likely be a good idea not to mention this to her, but if you ever find yourself in the Athens Story, seek him out and bring him to her. She needs to see him again, for her sanity more than anything else."

"O-oh. I can do that," Will said, though he wasn't really sure why Rachel's brother would be in another Story.

Now The Huntsman was patting him on the head like he was some sort of a dog, not really paying attention to Will. His attention was fixed out the door, staring at nothing. Apparently, that behavior was concerning to Red as well; she frowned and tugged on his sleeve. "*Oncle?*" she said.

"*Oui?*" He turned back to her, raising his eyebrows.

"Is something wrong?" Will and Red said at the same time.

He forced a smile to them. "Oh, no. Nothing. It is all well. If you'll excuse me …"

Red grabbed his arm before he could walk off. "Oh no you don't," she said in warning. "You cannot leave us with that. There is something wrong, or you would not have stared at nothing like that. You *never* do that. Tell me what is wrong!"

The Huntsman looked pained. "My abilities as a Guardian have not activated in years," he said softly. "And yet they did just now."

"What does that mean?" Red asked impatiently.

"It means …" The Huntsman looked at Red with distant eyes. "That someone has used magic on Rachel and Guy."

Chapter 16: The Queen of Evil

"All this for some blasted herbs?" Guy complained as they tramped through the chilly forest a few minutes after they'd left the cabin. "I'd simply settle for unflavored soup!"

"It's not for the soup," Rachel said. "It's for Will. And I didn't invite you along. If you want to complain to someone, direct it at The Huntsman for making you come."

To be honest, her desire to go find the herbs was more from a strong desire to get out of that cabin and think and less about helping Will—though that was a positive side to it. It made her seem less selfish to think like that. The Huntsman had rubbed salt in an old wound, yet it hurt as much as if it had only been yesterday. Even without the threat of Ewan not remembering her, Rachel wasn't sure if she would've been enthusiastic about seeing him. Their parting had not been sweet, and she wasn't sure if she wanted to see him. After all, the only one to blame for his banishment was *him*.

The silence between her and Guy had stretched on for too long, and Rachel shrugged. "Well, I wouldn't. There's nothing worse than flavorless soup."

Scanning the ground to avoid looking at Guy, she saw some thyme growing and knelt beside it. She started ripping it out of the ground with uncalled-for fervor. Perhaps unwisely, Guy bent down beside Rachel and fixed her with a serious look. "I heard about your brother," he said simply.

Rachel refused to meet his eyes. "So?" she answered sharply.

"So ..." Guy seemed undeterred by her cold response. "Perhaps it would help if you talked about it?"

"Oh, not you too," Rachel retorted, stuffing the herbs into a bag supplied by The Huntsman and standing. "I don't need everyone telling me I'm wrong and they're right. Why do you all think I need your advice? How do any of you know how I feel?"

Guy raised his eyebrows in an infuriating way. "We can't know how you feel if you don't tell us," he replied lightly.

"Oh, shove off," Rachel said, walking away. To her chagrin, he followed her. When he stopped walking, she thought she heard another set of footsteps halt a split second after Guy did. "Did you hear that?"

"I couldn't hear anything over your complaining." Guy crossed his arms, looking down at her. Somehow, that just made him seem even more annoying.

Rachel sighed. "Why are you being so annoying?"

"Because we care about you, Rachel," Guy said. "You are The Story's best hope of survival. If you aren't focused, then the rest of us may as well just bow down to the intruder and beg for mercy. Is that what you want?"

"Why do you care?" Rachel yelled, not caring that her voice carried through the trees. "You're a villain! Aren't you supposed to want the destruction of everybody? What do you hope to gain from coming with us?"

Guy looked away, his gaze far away. "Repentance," he answered softly. "For crimes you cannot imagine."

She stared at him. "I don't know what you mean."

When he turned back to her, there was a slightly bitter smile on his face. "You weren't intended to," he said. "Forgive me, but if you wish to hide something from me, than you can hardly complain that I do the same to you."

In an effort to calm herself, Rachel took a deep breath. She kept walking, trying to ignore an odd, shivery feeling going up and down her spine. "You are a most annoying person," she told him at last.

"Am I?" Guy shrugged. "Or is it just because you know I'm right?"

Rachel sighed. "How can you twist my words into that?" she asked in annoyance. "You're not right. And someone is following us," she added as she knelt down beside a patch of wild rosemary.

"What?" Guy knelt down beside her, staring. "Who?"

Rachel shook her head. "I don't know—yet. But I will find out. I think whoever it is might be messing with us."

"In what way?"

"Our emotions. Can't you feel it?" she asked, trying to keep herself from snapping at him. "We're being toyed with. You might as well come out!" she added in a yell. To Guy, she whispered, "Calendula. By that tree. Hurry."

As a black-garbed figure emerged from the trees, Guy slipped behind Rachel to do as he was told. For the first time, she was glad he was there. They needed the calendula for Will, or he would die.

Their stalker was an ancient-looking woman, with wrinkles flowing down her pale face like a waterfall. Black eyes peered out from beneath the wrinkles. A prominent, pointed nose halted only inches from Rachel's face, the woman's hunched back taking several inches from her height. Grey hair was clumped together down her back; her breath smelled bad and seemed mixed with ... apples?

When the woman spoke, Rachel saw that she was missing multiple teeth. "Pretty, pretty child," she cackled, her German accent weighing down on her words. "Why do you fear me?" A crooked finger bubbled up with warts was extended forward, as if to stroke Rachel's cheek.

Swiftly, Rachel stepped back two paces and drew her sword. "What do you want?" she asked. "What are you doing to us?"

132

The old woman cackled again. "I am not doing anything to you!" she said sneeringly. "It is Morpheus who is causing you such pain, little one! I am simply exposing you to the pain, opening a door that you would normally keep closed."

Rachel nearly jumped out of her skin when something rubbed against her arm, but it was only Guy, coming to stand beside her. Unlike Rachel, his sword remained sheathed. "Who are you?" he said calmly.

The old woman leered at him. "Guy of Gisborne," she said, her voice softening to almost a purr. "My, my, you are as handsome as the legends say. Why do you choose this side? Do you imagine that you will be accepted by them, even after the sins you have committed come to light?"

Guy stiffened visibly. "I don't know what you're talking about."

"Pah, pathetic," she spat at him. As Rachel watched mutely, her eyes widening, the old hag started to morph before their eyes. A wave of raven hair covered the grey, her posture straightened, the wrinkles smoothed into perfect skin. Chiseled cheekbones, fine lines, and a flawless face replaced the old crone from before. The only evidence that it was the same woman were the black eyes and the pointed nose. She appeared to be fifty years younger. "You really are an imbecile. Pity ... you are a handsome lad."

"Leave him alone," Rachel said, but her voice came out only as a squeak. The woman was intimidating, to say the least, particularly since she had a good head and a half of height over Rachel. She might have been worse than the Wolf.

A thudding sound caught Rachel's attention, and she swung around just in time to see the Wolf himself come lumbering out of the forest, charging at Guy. The knight turned just in time to get a forearm to the chest and went

133

flying back to the trees. Rachel tried to swing her sword at the Wolf, but the woman caught her wrist and jerked her back. "Do you not know who I am?" she asked as she wrestled Rachel under control, wrapping an arm around her throat. She was far stronger than she looked. "I am Mal, Queen of Evil."

"From Snow White's Story," Rachel rasped out. "Let go of me!"

"Wouldn't it be ironic, for you to fall under the same spell your brother is so fond of?" Mal mused. She hardly seemed to be breaking a sweat, even holding the struggling, squirming Rachel tightly to her.

The Wolf stood over Guy, snarling at him. The knight was looking up at him, his eyes narrowed, but not moving, half-crouched on the ground. "Please," Rachel choked out. "Let him go, if you won't release me."

Mal shook her head, still watching Guy. "Why would I let such a handsome boy escape?" she said flirtatiously. "Do I look like a fool to you?"

The fury on Guy's face seemed to take away all his good looks. He lashed out at the Wolf, burying his blade deep into the monster's chest. The Wolf gave a howl of pain and staggered backwards, blood covering his brown fur. However, when Guy attempted to reach Rachel, the Wolf grabbed his arm and dug his claws into the man's skin. Guy cried out in pain.

"No!" Rachel struggled, managing to elbow Mal in the gut. The woman staggered back with a wheeze, and Rachel tumbled to the ground. Her breath came in ragged gasps as she tried desperately to regain her footing before the Wolf could finish Guy off.

But things just weren't destined to fall in Rachel's favor. A swift kick in the side from Mal sent her sprawling, and the Queen of Evil knelt down beside her. "Ah, my darling," she said sweetly. "Did you really think you would get away so easily?"

Before Rachel could even attempt to rise, Mal leaned down and touched her forehead. "Good night," she crooned ...

And everything went black.

Chapter 17: Fight or Flight

When Rachel collapsed, limp as a rag doll, Guy froze momentarily. Magic still disturbed him, and he had a feeling it always would. If he managed to escape his present situation, at least. He could almost take a detached view of things, particularly of his own fate, but Rachel's ...

Mal knelt down to scoop up Rachel, and Guy instantly reacted without even considering it. He slammed his fist into the Wolf's snout, causing the beast to recoil and release him. Once he was free, he sprinted towards Mal and Rachel, tackling the Queen. She gave a shriek as he slammed her down, but he didn't stay in place for long. Once she was down and away from Rachel, he swiftly grabbed the blonde girl, throwing her over his shoulder as he scrambled to his feet and ran. It wasn't the most comfortable position for either of them, but he didn't have time to think.

Thudding from behind him indicated that the Wolf was just on his heels. Guy's breath came in ragged gasps as he sprinted, fear shooting through him. But not fear for himself—fear for Rachel. Fear for The Story. If she died, then ... what he had done would never be fixed; or, perhaps not fixed, but *repaired*.

"Kill him!" Mal screeched from behind him. The Wolf snarled in response, grabbing at Guy's back. Claws dug in, tearing through his shirt, drawing blood, but he didn't stop. Even when the claws tore at his skin, he kept running, carrying the deadweight of the Guardian with him. Adrenaline kept the pain at bay, but it would only last him for so long. He had to be back at The Huntsman's home before then.

The trees slapped at him as he ran, pulling at his hair, tearing through his arms. Roots threatened to trip him, and the thudding of the Wolf's loping behind seemed to dog at his steps, threatening him. One misstep, and both Guy and Rachel would be at those monsters' mercy.

And he knew they had none.

The forest path was barely able to be described as such. Littered with pebbles, broken twigs, and holes, it was a hazard in of itself. Guy, for the first time in ages, found himself praying, desperately hoping they'd make it. The chances were slim, but he had to hope for something.

The trees began thinning out as he sprinted, his arms aching, his breath coming in ragged gasps. *Only a little more ...* His feet pounded, feeling as if they were becoming as if they could drop out from beneath him at any second. Even worse, Rachel was starting to thrash around and groan, making it difficult to hold on to her. "Would you just be still?" he growled, struggling to hold her in place. It was slowing him down.

"You can't run forever, Gisborne!" Mal snapped at him.

He didn't waste breath responding to her. A stitch was beginning to appear in his side, and he prayed he would reach safety before that became a bigger problem. Sweat beaded down his brow, and his throat felt unusually dry.

"Look out!" Someone tackled him without warning just as the Wolf lunged, flying over their heads. Without having realizing it, Guy had reached The Huntsman's yard, and Will Scarlet had just saved his life. The irony of that situation was not lost on Guy, who had no time to thank the outlaw. Instead, he had to cast about for Rachel, seeing her unconscious form sprawled on the lawn a few feet away from him.

Mal stopped at the edge of The Huntsman's lawn; the Queen lit her hand with a fireball. "Surrender," she snapped at

Will and Guy. From the other side of them, the Wolf approached on all fours, snarling.

"Where's The Huntsman?" Guy demanded, pulling Rachel closer to him. The girl slapped at him, trying to get him away for some unknown reason. Her eyes remained stubbornly closed.

"He told me to come out and help you," Will said, staring at Mal. "That lady has a fireball."

"Yes, yes she does," Guy said with a trace of annoyance. "Did you come out just to tell me that?"

Will shrugged. "Is she going to throw it?"

Mal stared at them. "Are you thick in the head, boy?" she asked him. The Wolf growled, but he too seemed puzzled by Will's behavior.

Will frowned. "That's rude," he told her. "And for your information, the only thing I was doing … was stalling."

With a solid *smack*, a crossbow bolt slammed into the Wolf's back, sending him staggering a few paces. "Load it!" The Huntsman yelled. Turning slightly, Guy saw both Red and her uncle standing on the porch. However, Red wasn't loading the crossbow he'd handed to her …

Mal moved to throw the fireball, but Red was just a tiny bit faster. Her club flew through the air, and landed with a solid, meaty *smack* on Mal's forehead. The Queen gave a screech of pain before dropping like a stone.

The Wolf, blood streaming down his back, staggered to his feet, snarling at Guy, Will, and Rachel. Will scrambled to his feet, raising his sword, his hand shaking. "H-Huntsman?" he said, his voice trembling slightly.

The Huntsman leveled his crossbow at Mal, who was trying to stand, dazed. Red was now reloading his original bow, tugging at the string. "Unless you want your Lady to perish, Wolf, I would advise backing away from them," he said.

Although it was evident the Wolf wanted to tear Guy's throat out, The Huntsman's threat seemed to halt him, at least for now. Still, furious eyes gazed hungrily at Guy. "Back," The Huntsman snapped off.

"Wolf!" Mal said, finally regaining her feet. A lump was forming on her forehead, where Red had hit her with the club. "We are leaving."

The Wolf growled at her. "Leaving? I tasted the boy's blood," he said, leering at Guy. "I want more."

"You will wait," Mal said sternly, raising her arms. She gave Guy a wink. "This is not over, my handsome knight. We'll meet again soon."

She spoke a word in German, and Guy doubled over, feeling as if all the air had been sucked from his lungs. When he could breathe semi-normally again, he looked up. Both the Wolf and Mal had disappeared, as if they'd never existed.

Guy was beginning to despise magic.

The Huntsman limped down to Guy and Will, noticing how Guy held the unconscious Rachel in his arms. "What happened?" he asked quietly, kneeling beside them.

Will rolled onto his back. "Nothing good," he groaned, blood seeping from his injuries.

Guy looked at The Huntsman with a touch of desperation. "Can something be done for her?" he asked, looking down at the girl.

The Huntsman took in a long, slow breath before standing up. He picked Will up in the process, and the outlaw frowned but didn't protest. "Come inside," was all the man said before making his way to the house.

As much as Guy wanted to berate him for his lack of information, he reluctantly followed The Huntsman into the cabin, carrying Rachel in his arms. The young woman was still thrashing and fighting, making strange choking noises in the back of her throat. That was making things difficult in carrying her in there.

Still, he somehow made it through the door and into the house without dropping the Guardian, and once he was there, The Huntsman took her from him. She still thrashed and struggled. For some reason, that gave Guy a strange sense of satisfaction. Rachel hadn't been struggling to escape from his grasp. She simply didn't know what she was doing.

Will was in one of the chairs next to the table, his injuries now an ugly red and leaking something that wasn't blood. The boy managed a faint smile when Guy entered the room, which meant he really must have been struggling. He probably never would have smiled at Guy in his right mind.

The Huntsman took Rachel to a separate room before returning, only to walk into the kitchen in the process. Red sat at the table, rubbing her ankle while watching the other two. "You did well to survive," she said, and it took Guy a moment to realize she was speaking to him.

"I hardly did anything," Guy replied. The Huntsman had taken Rachel's bag, which had the herbs in it, including the calendula. "I had to be rescued like some sort of a damsel, by an outlaw. The irony is remarkable."

"It's not so bad, getting rescued by me," Will protested, his hand idly laying atop his injuries.

"We are enemies, you and I," Guy said curtly. "Perhaps allies at the moment, but never friends."

"That's harsh," Will answered.

"Harsh, perhaps, but true," Guy retorted. "And don't bother pretending we're the best of friends, Scarlet. I know you despise me as much as I despise you."

Will pursed his lips. "Perhaps," he said. "But ... remember what I said last night."

A grunt was the only response Guy gave, for the moment. He didn't want to get into that in front of Red, who was watching them curiously. "Something wrong?" Red asked, the tiniest hint of a mocking smile pointed in Guy's direction.

"No, of course not," Guy said, with a smooth smile that was really resisting the temptation to hit both Red and Will. They seemed intent on mocking him, and he wished they'd simply leave him alone.

It seemed that wasn't what was meant to be. They both looked piercingly at him and he wanted nothing more than to retreat to one of the other rooms. If it hadn't been for Rachel, he would have. But he wanted to know what was ailing the young woman and why she'd suddenly become unresponsive.

Will leaned back, putting his hand to his chest. When he pulled it away, it was sticky with blood. "This whole situation is incredibly uncomfortable," he said.

"In more ways than one," Red muttered, tapping her fingers against the table.

Guy inclined his head slightly towards her, an indication that she was right. The young French woman raised her eyebrows at him. None of them spoke again, though all three of them ended up tapping their fingers against the table when The Huntsman failed to come out within a few minutes.

The silence was interrupted a few minutes later by a blood-curling shriek. Guy instinctively covered his ears with his hands, cringing at the noise. "What the devil is that?" he said, grimacing.

Red flinched. "I ..."

141

The Huntsman burst out of the kitchen and moved into the room he'd put Rachel in. Will covered his head with his hands. "I should've stayed in Sherwood Forest!"

"I wish you had," Guy shot back, standing up and going towards the room that Rachel was in. Before he could open the door, The Huntsman opened it and stepped outside. "Why was she screaming?"

The Huntsman sighed, motioning him back towards the table. Reluctantly, Guy sat down. "Well?" he said impatiently.

The Huntsman sat down beside Guy and rubbed his chin. "I am afraid that I have little experience in the ways of sleeping curses," he said. "I need to know if anything Mal said indicated what kind of a spell that was cast. Did she say anything before casting the spell on Rachel?"

Guy scrunched up his face as he thought. "She said something about it being ironic. And something about Morpheus?"

The Huntsman stood and spat a word out in French that was obviously not flattering. Before Guy could ask him what was the matter, the man had moved into the kitchen and returned with a bowl of some kind of paste in it. The Huntsman tugged out Will's chair a little more before slathering the paste onto his fingers. He proceeded to apply it to Will's wounds.

The outlaw hissed the instant The Huntsman's fingers came into contact with his skin. "By heaven, that hurts like the devil himself was biting me!" he complained.

"Relax," was The Huntsman's advice. "There is some Guardian magic at work here. It will heal the wounds and purge the poison that foul woman applied to the Wolf's claws. It may hurt for a little while, but it will get better shortly."

Will gave a smile that came across as more of a grimace. "I hope it's sooner rather than later," he muttered.

"Perhaps." The Huntsman didn't seem to be in the mood for any joking around, and ignored Will's attempt at humor.

Guy came back to a more important point, for him. "How do we wake up Rachel?"

The Huntsman shook his head. "I personally do not know."

"So what?" Guy said, half-rising from his seat. "We allow her to sleep the rest of her days away? What is there to be gained from that? There *must* be a way to break this sleeping magic!"

"I did not say there was no way," The Huntsman answered, rising from his position beside Will. The boy's chest was slathered in the strange, green-colored paste. "I simply said that *I* cannot break it. That does not mean that somebody else cannot."

"Then where do we go, to get this spell broken?" Will questioned through gritted teeth.

"To her brother," the man replied. "Morpheus. I will make a Story door for you to go there. In the end, though, you will have to be careful around him."

Guy gave a small grimace. "Indeed." There was no need for The Huntsman to explain *why*, that was for certain.

It evidently got Will and Red curious, for now they were both looking at Guy. However, he simply glared at them, clearly telling them to mind their own business. Will grinned impishly, as if he planned to ask anyway, but The Huntsman interrupted. "It would likely be best if you moved as soon as possible. If the intruder sent Mal and the Wolf, it could mean that he may attempt some form of attack on Morpheus to prevent him from waking Rachel. You must leave and go there." He knelt beside Red, removing the bandages from her ankle.

"But what about you? You can come with us," Will suggested.

The Huntsman smiled mirthlessly as he applied the paste to Red's ankle. "A cripple like me?" he said. "You flatter me, young Will, but I would not be a proper companion to you." He looked piercingly at Red, who was very carefully trying to avoid his gaze. "Is there something you want to tell me?"

"I would like to go with them, Uncle Charles," Red told him softly, grimacing as the paste slipped into her injuries. "I cannot stay here when I know there are such terrible things happening in The Story. Will you permit me to go, *Oncle*?"

"Much as it grieves me to let you, for fear that I may never see you again, you possess the stubbornness of your grandmother," The Huntsman answered with a good deal of affection. With his clean hand, he touched her cheek gently. "You understand the risks, Red?"

"Of course," she said, looking offended. "I am not a child anymore."

The Huntsman ducked his head slightly as he wrapped her ankle once more. "I am foolish to forget," he said. "Forgive me, Red. You are free to leave, if you wish. Do know that it is likely that you will not return here until you succeed."

"I wish you would come," Red whispered, brushing at her cheeks with a hint of annoyance.

"Ahh, but you know that is impossible," he answered in a similar tone, gently pushing her hair away from her face before standing. "Guy, would you come and gather some food with me?"

144

Although Guy knew that was simply a fancy way of saying he wanted to speak with him in private, he nodded and stood. The two men went into the kitchen, where The Huntsman started digging around in his cupboards for food. He handed Guy a satchel—the same one they'd used to carry their gathered herbs—and instructed him, rather abruptly, to start finding anything he thought would be useful and put it in the bag.

Guy silently did as he was told, glancing back at him once. "Did you want to talk with me about something?" he asked after a few moments of silence.

The Huntsman turned slightly to look at him. "*Oui*," he said. "You know why Morpheus—or Ewan Andric, as I know him by—will not be fond of you?"

A cold hand clutched at Guy's heart. "How much do you know?" he asked.

The Huntsman shrugged. "Enough. Only what I was told by Ewan himself. But enough."

"And do you hold me accountable? Despise me for it?" Guy went on.

"Not entirely, no. As a Guardian, I understand that the impulses of the character that you are can be difficult to stop," The Huntsman said. "However, you understand that what you did is verging on unforgivable. If the young Lady Andric learns what you did, it may very well cause her to send you away."

"I shall deal with that when it comes," Guy replied. "Leave that to me."

"Indeed," The Huntsman said, just a little amusement. "I wish you luck in your quest when she finds out, then."

Guy sent him an annoyed look. "She will not find out."

145

"Do you think that Ewan will really hesitate in telling her?" The Huntsman questioned, though his voice was significantly quieter and gentler. "You are fooling yourself if you do."

Guy smiled, though it was utterly bitter. "I'm afraid you're right," he admitted in the same soft voice. "But I shall deal with it when it comes."

"Very well," The Huntsman said, laying a gentle hand on Guy's shoulder. "I wish you luck in your journey, then, and hope that it does not come to an end sooner than you had anticipated."

"I believe in Rachel's sense of fairness," Guy said, looking up. "I believe that she will judge me fairly."

"Do you think that fairness comes into play with this kind of a sin?" The Huntsman asked, shaking his head. "Fair or not, the odds are high that she will hate you."

Guy bit down on his lip. "Thank you for your optimism," he said stiffly, shouldering the bag of supplies.

"You are most welcome," The Huntsman said with a chuckle. "Shall we return to the others, then?"

"If you are finished speaking with me, then yes," Guy replied. The two men made their way back into the other room, where Guy was vaguely amused to see Will trying to look as if he hadn't wanted to know what they'd been saying. The boy rested his chin on his fist. "Ready?" was all he said.

"If you two are," Guy answered, glancing over at Red. The young French woman shrugged in response, which he took to mean she was ready. "You carry the bags. I'll take Rachel."

"Fair enough," Will said with a slight inclination of his head. He took the two satchels from Guy, while Red retrieved the supplies they'd received from the Merry Men. The Huntsman took Guy into Rachel's room, where the young

146

woman had switched from screaming to muttering and groaning under her breath. Guy slid his arm under her knees and the other under her shoulders; with only the slightest grunt, he lifted her out of the bed and into his arms.

He took Rachel out into the dining room, where Red had put on her scarlet hood, and Will had buckled both his sword sheath and quiver on his hips. His bow was slung over his shoulder. The boy's eyes remained on Rachel for several seconds, struggling and twisting in Guy's arms. "Is she ... alright?" he asked tentatively.

"We'll find out when we see Morpheus," Guy replied. "And if he can't tell us, then we'll simply look for someone who can. Giving up on her is not an option."

Will nodded. "Right. I'm ready."

Red hesitated before spinning, and throwing her arms around The Huntsman's neck. She whispered in French to him, and he responded in like before kissing the top of her head. When she pulled away, Guy had to pretend he didn't notice the tear sliding down her cheek. "I am ready," she said softly, but gruffly. The glare she sent at Guy seemed to be daring him to say something about her crying.

To spare both her pride and his own discomfort, he said nothing. Instead of responding to her, he turned back to The Huntsman. "You can make the door for us, correct?" he asked.

The Huntsman nodded and squeezed his eyes shut. After a decent period of time, a door materialized into sight, in the middle of the dining room. The Huntsman opened his eyes and gave them a thin smile. "I think I shall have to sleep for a century after all this magicking," he said jokingly. "*Au revoir*, and take care. I shall miss you, Red, but I have no doubt that you and the others shall save The Story."

"*Merci*," Red mumbled, looking as if she wished he hadn't spoken. She stared down at her feet and wouldn't meet anyone else's eyes.

"Good-bye," Will said. "Thank you for all the help you've given to us. Chances are that we wouldn't have survived without you."

"Ahh, you are resourceful," The Huntsman said, waving his hand. "I simply helped where I could, but you would have lived without me. Take care of that young lady." He pointed at Rachel. "She is strong, but she will not be able to do it alone."

"It is our pleasure," Guy answered quietly.

Red gave The Huntsman a final embrace before hurrying through his door. Before she'd fully gone through, Guy thought he heard a small sob. Judging from the discomfort on Will's face, the outlaw had heard the same thing. Will gave an awkward wave to The Huntsman before following Red through the door.

Guy glanced over at The Huntsman as he stood in front of the door. "Will is right, you know. We would have died without your aid. Particularly me."

"You are a good man, Guy of Gisborne," The Huntsman said. "I wish you luck."

"We'll need all the luck we can get," Guy answered, and went through the door with the still-struggling Rachel in his arms.

Chapter 18: Morpheus, God of Sleep

When Guy and Rachel came through the door, Will met them with a confused expression as he looked about. The place they were in was like nothing he had ever seen before, and he could tell from Guy's expression that he was as impressed as Will felt.

They were in a dark alleyway, with smooth cobblestones beneath their feet. Red leaned against the wall of a nearby building, watching them and the street at the same time. When Will looked at her, she stood up a little straighter. "I believe we are in Athens," she said.

"Athens?" Will questioned, scratching at his chest with a pained look on his face. The blood had dried, rendering it quite stiff and itchy.

"Greece," Red said. "Likely the home of this Morpheus we have been sent to look for. According to my uncle, he is a minor god. We shall have some trouble finding him, I believe ..."

"Trouble or not, we must find him." Guy spoke with confidence and cast a rather dark glare at the young woman.

Red shook her head slightly. "I did not say we wouldn't. I just fear what will happen if *someone else* finds him first," she reminded him.

Before an argument could break out between the two of them, Will spoke up. "One thing is plain, at least to me," he said. "If we don't get moving, we definitely won't get to him in time." He hesitated for a beat. "Does anyone know how to speak Greece?"

"*Greek*," Red corrected him. "And no. But we shall find out if that is important. Come along."

Thank God, it was nighttime, and there weren't many people walking the streets. Torches illuminated both sides of the road, as well as white temples lined with columns. The only people who walked the streets wore strange white bedsheets and gave Will and his friends a wide berth. A creepy silence seemed to be casting an eerie spell over the entire city.

As the group made their way through the streets, Will became aware that, no matter how many turns they took and how many white temples they passed, someone followed them. It was a good distance back, always hidden by the light from the torches, but in the ten minutes they'd been walking, their stalker was always there.

Guy glanced back once. "I think someone is back there," he said quietly, shifting Rachel into a more comfortable position in his arms. "Following us."

Will gave a barely-perceptible nod. "I thought as much. That confirms it. What do we do?"

Red stepped in front of Guy, blocked by his greater height and bulk. She walked there until they were out of the torchlight, at which point she slipped into the shadows. Even with her red hood, Will could hardly see her. Guy and Will kept walking, understanding what her admittedly-risky plan was.

It all happened in seconds. As they kept going, Will heard a startled cry and a dull *thump*. Both he and Guy swung around and saw Red standing over a semi-conscious man, also clad in that strange white blanket. Why was everyone wearing them?

The man groaned, his bald head already sporting a lump from Red's club. The young woman crouched over him, still clutching the club. Will laid his hand on the pommel of his sword, an unspoken threat, but not drawn yet. "Why were you following us?" he asked, keeping his voice calm.

The man sat up slightly. "You are strangers," he said, making no move to stand yet. "I have orders to follow all strangers who come to Athens."

"Follow them? For what purpose?" Guy demanded, with a less congenial tone than Will.

"To see who comes," the man answered, his eyes rather glazed. He tried his best to focus on Guy, and his gaze slid down to Rachel, her pale arm hanging down limply. "By the beard of Zeus! What color are that girl's eyes?"

"What c-color?" Will stammered.

"Are they blue? A clear blue?" the man pressed on, ignoring the scowl Red was directing at him.

Guy nodded slowly. "Yes. You know Morpheus, don't you?"

The bald man went to stand, and Will reluctantly helped him up. Red continued to shoot him menacing looks, which seemed to be terrifying him. Will diplomatically stepped between them. "Can you take us to him?" Will said, hoping against hope that the man could actually be trusted and wouldn't lead them into some sort of a trap. That would just be bad altogether. He supposed if the worst happened, Red could just hit him with her club again.

The man nodded, enthusiastic now that Red was separated from him. Will didn't have the heart to tell him that she could probably lunge around him and still get to the man. "Follow me," he said, and started leading the way down the street.

It occurred to Will for the first time that the man was speaking English, not Greek. However, just as he had with the talking wolf, Guy seemed to take the whole thing in stride. In a way, Will was envious of him. Nothing seemed to bother him, not even running for his life from the savage Wolf, while Will felt as if he were drowning. The entire thing just baffled him entirely, and nobody—aside from The Huntsman—had bothered to try and explain it to him. Maybe he should have just stayed in Sherwood Forest ...

He was shaken out of that particular depressing thought by the man starting off. When his two companions followed the bald fellow, Will heaved a sigh and trailed along as well. His chest still itched like mad and he desperately wanted to take off the bandages to reach them more easily. However, now was certainly not the time.

They walked for what felt like an eternity. By that time, Will grew less annoyed and more bored. Each temple looked identical—brightly lit, white, with several stairs leading up to the open area within—and it was almost dizzying. Really, all Will wanted was to sit down and rip the bandages from his chest.

Finally, they came to a temple that didn't resemble the others. Granted, it was still white, with the same columns and steps as the others, but it was significantly smaller, and dark. There were no torches along the front of it, giving the temple a look of gloom and eeriness. It took Will a moment to realize their guide was hurrying up the steps, and Will grimaced. "Oh no," he said. "He doesn't mean for us to go *inside*, does he?"

Guy ignored him and mounted the stairs, but Red remained with Will. Perhaps that was just so she could give him a strange look. "Is there something wrong with that?" she questioned.

"That's a *pagan* temple," Will said. "If there was anything that my mum taught me, it was that there's just one God, and that one of the Ten Commandments says not to have any gods before Him."

"Does one of those same Commandments not say that you should not steal?" Red asked, raising her eyebrows at him. When Will blushed, the young woman gave a sigh. "You are not *worshipping* Morpheus, Will."

"But still ..." Will looked doubtful.

"For heaven's sake, Will, would you rather wait outside while myself and Guy deal with Morpheus?" Red snapped in frustration. "We do not have the time for this."

As much as Will hated to admit it, he knew she was right. When she swept past him, her red cloak slapping around her, he reluctantly followed her inside. The darkened temple was devoid of furnishing, but there were people—at least thirty of them—laying on the floor, sleeping. Surreptitiously, Will Crossed himself as he trailed along behind the others.

The small group stopped at the back of the temple, where a doorway was secreted in the wall, only visible by the small crack of light around the sides. Their guide motioned them back, and he went forward alone, knocking tentatively on the door. There was a mumbled response from within, the words lost in Greek, and their guide spoke in like. Moments later, he stepped aside. "Go in," he said.

The three companions exchanged suddenly-nervous looks, no one willing to face the voice beyond the curtain. Finally, Red tossed her raven hair at them and pushed past their guide, into the room. When she moved, Will and Guy glanced at each other, a little ashamed, before going after Red.

The room beyond was strange looking. There were three sets of two beds on top of each other, with barely enough room between each other and the ceiling. Several candles illuminated the room, which had been causing the eerie light from within the temple.

Perhaps the creepiest part of the room was the man standing in the middle of it. He stood about a half a head taller than Will, clad entirely in a black cloak, his face covered by a cowl. His muscular arms were crossed over his chest; thin, red lips the only part of his face visible beneath the cowl.

For several long moments, the group regarded the man as he watched them. The silence stretched on, awkward and ... well, silent. Finally, the man's deep voice rang out through the room. "Welcome to Athens."

"*Merci*," Red said. "You are Morpheus, are you not? Ewan Andric."

There was just a second's hesitation before Morpheus reached up and brushed his cowl from his head. He revealed pale-white skin, clear-blue eyes, and tousled raven hair that indicated a younger man than his deep voice had led Will to believe—probably somewhere in his early twenties. "I am. And you must be Little Red Riding Hood."

"You remember?" she questioned, frowning.

"You threatened to brain me with a club," Morpheus said ruefully. "And you were *ten*. You were, hands-down, the scariest thing I had to deal with as a Guardian. Of course I remember you."

Red looked away, blushing. That made Guy raise his eyebrows, for some reason, but he didn't have long to enjoy the expression. Morpheus swung his gaze to Guy, and his icy eyes became considerably more hostile. Will was just grateful that look wasn't directed at himself. "Guy of Gisborne," Morpheus said quietly. "I never thought I'd see the day that you would step foot in my house. Holding my sister in your arms. You have no shame, do you?"

Guy straightened his posture, maintaining a neutral expression on his face. An enemy of Will's or not, Will couldn't help but feel bad for him. "I don't know about shame, Morpheus, but your sister was almost abducted by Queen Mal and the Big Bad Wolf," Guy replied. "I nearly died trying to save her. Think of me what you will, but I brought her here to you because she is under a sleeping curse that you are apparently fond of."

Morpheus looked from Rachel to Guy, his face unreadable. Then he reached forward and took Rachel from Guy, holding her gently. A single tear tracked its way down his cheek before he took her to one of the beds and laid her down. Will thought he detected a look of satisfaction on Guy's face when the Guardian kept struggling, even in Morpheus's arms. "Can you fix it?" Will felt he had to ask.

"Can I?" Morpheus turned, brushing the tear from his cheek. He managed a smile at Will. "Of course I can. Sleeping spells are my specialty, if they don't involve true love's kiss. In fact, I've already enacted the spell necessary to wake her up. And you are …?" There was a slightly strange expression on Morpheus's face, as if his question was simply a trick question.

"Will. Will Scarlet," he answered. "Thank you for helping Rachel."

Now there was definitely amusement twitching the end of Morpheus's lips. "You're thanking me for helping my own sister?" he said. "You're weird." With bad grace, he turned to the others, motioning to the beds. "Make yourselves comfortable, I guess. Do you want anything to eat?"

Will sat down and started tugging his shirt off. The bandages had dried to his chest, and he wanted to take them off. Morpheus saw him and came over, untying the knot The Huntsman had tied and helping him remove the bandages. Although scars remained, it was as if he'd had the injuries for months, not less than a few hours. "Good heavens, what happened?" he wondered aloud, feeling the injuries tentatively. They were still sticky from the paste that had been applied.

"Someone used powerful Guardian magic on these," Morpheus said. "They were poisoned, from the looks of them, but the poison was purged. Weird ... the magic should have fixed all outward signs of a wound ..." He trailed off with a frown, fixing Will with yet another strange look.

A groan interrupted their conversation. "Oww ... where am I?"

Immediately, Morpheus whipped himself from Will's side and hurried to Rachel, who was trying to sit up. "Rach, Rach, are you okay?" he asked, in a slightly panicked voice.

The Guardian took a few seconds to focus on him. When she did, her eyes went wide and she threw her arms around his neck, bursting into tears. "Ewan! You remember me! You know who I am!"

Looking bemused, Morpheus nevertheless put his arms around her and held her close. "Rachel ... of course I do. I could never forget you forever, sis ..."

When Rachel raised her eyes to him, they were rimmed with red and tears still streamed down her cheeks. "I've missed you. I've missed you so much."

Morpheus brushed the tears from her cheeks and leaned his forehead against hers. "I've missed you too, Rachel. More than you could possibly know."

"I think I know," Rachel answered, and buried her face in his shoulder once more. It seemed as if they would never part.

Chapter 19: A Sister's Fury

Rachel and Morpheus remained in an embrace for so long, Will began to feel incredibly awkward. When they finally parted, Rachel rubbed her eyes and looked up at her brother. She looked more fragile and uncertain than Will had ever seen her before, but there was an unusual light in her eyes.

Morpheus pulled away slightly, brushing a curl of Rachel's hair from her eyes. "Rach," he said. "How did he get here?"

"The intruder?" Rachel asked, rubbing her eyes. "He attacked me. Came to our island and forced me to remove the covering over the book. I followed him inside and now I think he's gathering an army to take over."

"Oh, I *know* he's gathering an army to take over," Morpheus said wryly. "He tried to recruit me. He didn't realize who I was, I guess."

"It would seem not," Will said, trying to get them to remember he was there.

Rachel physically jumped and looked at them. "Oh! Will! Guy ... Red? What are you doing here?"

"I chose to accompany you here," Red answered smoothly. "I trust you have no trouble with my presence?"

"N-no," Rachel stammered. "Of course not. You're most welcome to join us, if that's what you want."

"It is."

"W-well." Rachel smiled slightly awkwardly. "Welcome to the group, then."

"*Merci.*" Will couldn't decide if Red was enjoying the situation or not. Whatever the case, the flat expression on her face gave no indication of what could be going on beneath it.

Rachel stared at Red for several seconds, looking as if she were still dazed from her sleep. She rubbed her forehead. "Okay, then."

Morpheus eyed the rest of them as if they were intruding. Which, really, they probably were, but that was beside the point. "I guess you can stay the night," he said after a long moment. "If you want."

"I believe we could all use a rest," Red put in, casting a glance at the unhappy Guy. "If it is no trouble?"

"I guess not," Morpheus said, his hand still in his sister's. "I can make some food. If you're hungry."

"I am," Will said.

Morpheus nodded slowly, though he didn't look too happy about leaving his sister. He pulled away before looking at Red and Will. "You may as well make yourselves comfortable," he said. "If you're going to stay."

"Wait, Ewan," Rachel said, sitting up a little straighter. "I'm not ready for you to leave yet."

Morpheus glanced back at her. "Something you wanted to talk about?" he asked, looking a little amused.

"Y-yes," Rachel stammered out. "I wanted to ask you ... why."

"Why?" Morpheus's eyebrows shot up, but Will noticed that his amusement had swiftly departed.

Rachel stood up, tugging her blonde curls over her shoulder. "Yes—why. Why did you leave me? Why did you do something so stupid, that you knew would only result in you ending up here? You were selfish and stupid, and now I don't really have a brother."

"Rachel, please, not in front of them—"

"We're doing this now." Although Rachel was about a foot shorter than Ewan, maybe more, she still looked fearsome, glaring up at him. "Didn't you promise me something when our parents died? Do you remember that, Ewan?"

Morpheus stared at the floor. "Rachel, please—"

"Oh, of course you don't remember," Rachel said sarcastically. "Why should you? It was only the most important promise you made to your grieving little sister, when you were all I had left in the world. You promised me, Ewan! You said you would never leave me like they did! And they didn't even leave willingly, but you did. You can't tell me that you didn't know what would happen to you if you tried to save Achilles."

"Okay, I did know!" Ewan burst out, throwing his hands into the air in surrender. "Of course I knew! What did you want me to do? Ignore the situation where people were suffering? Just carry on, as if people weren't dying every day, uselessly? Is that what you wanted? A brother who turned a blind eye?"

"I wanted a brother who would actually have been around!" Rachel yelled. "Who keeps his word! What did it get you, Ewan? It got you here, in a worthless life, no better than the people you tried to 'save'. What good did it do you, Ewan?"

"It eased my conscience," Morpheus answered quietly. "And that's all that matters."

The heated argument was *really* making Will uncomfortable. However, the siblings didn't even seem to really notice the others were there. "Oh, is it all that matters?" Rachel said, her voice colder than ice. "I guess I don't matter, then."

"That's not what I meant!" Morpheus protested.

"You did say that easing your conscience was all that mattered," Rachel pointed out, raising her eyebrows.

Morpheus sighed. "You don't understand. I knew you wouldn't. You never did."

Rachel raised her eyes to him, her clear eyes cold as ice. "You *always* tell me that. Let me take a guess what you were trying to accomplish. You were trying to get yourself kicked out of the Guardians and written into The Story. That way, you didn't have to face the responsibility anymore. Am I right?"

Morpheus clenched his fists, straightening his back. "Fine! Yes. I wanted to get tossed out of the Guardians, no matter the cost. I couldn't do it anymore. I had to give Red back her basket so she could go get eaten by the Wolf! She was about ten years old, Rachel. Can you imagine how hard that was? You've never been in The Story before, Rach. You don't understand what it means."

Rachel put her hands on her hips. "Yes, I understand what it means," she shot back. "Do you think I'm stupid? Of course I feel horrible for them. Of *course* I want to help them. They're my friends. But does that mean I'm going to make a stupid stand that will only lose me the last member of my family I've got left?"

Ewan flinched. "It wasn't stupid—"

"Then what did it accomplish?" Rachel replied. "Did it get you anything? Did you save Achilles? No. He just got killed right afterwards. Bravo, Ewan. Well done. Lose your life and your sister all in one go, for one stupid stand that didn't get you or even Achilles anywhere."

Morpheus shrank away from her, an ashamed expression battling with a stubborn pride. "I did what I thought was right, Rachel. Someday, you might understand."

Rachel heaved a sigh. "It's always the same way for you, isn't it. You're always right and I never understand. I'm

160

not a child anymore, Ewan, in case you didn't notice. But you didn't, I guess."

Morpheus ran a hand through his hair in annoyance. "Oh, just shove off," he said irritably. "You're certainly acting like a child, aren't you? Grow up."

Rachel squared her shoulders, meeting his eyes with anger bright in her gaze. "Why did I ever think this was a good idea?" she said. "Coming to find you, hoping to see you again ... what did I picture, a fairytale meeting? I was stupid. I should've known you wouldn't even care."

"That's not fair," Morpheus protested. Will almost felt bad for Rachel's brother; she was bombarding him, giving him little chance of defending himself. Granted, his defenses and retorts weren't exactly endearing him to Rachel. "I love you, Rach. I'm so glad that you came back. I thank God for it."

"You thank God?" Will put in, trying to change the subject, trying to allay the siblings' fury at each other.

"Yeah." Morpheus looked at Will a little suspiciously. "Just because I have the title of a god doesn't mean that I don't believe in God. Anyway, the gods aren't really gods. We're as mortal as the next guy. In fact, we're basically sorcerers with varying strengths. Put me up against a sorcerer like Merlin and he'd probably have me hanging on his wall as a trophy."

"Stop changing the subject." Apparently, Rachel hadn't exactly appreciated Will's interruption, and he shrank back. "Why? Why did you do this?"

"Because I couldn't take it anymore!" Morpheus cried. "These people needed death. Not just their repeating death, but something more permanent. They have no prospect of getting to Heaven, Rach. They just get stuck here, dying over and over again, and if they don't die how they're 'supposed' to die, then they undergo Final Death, and heaven only knows what happens to them *there!*"

Rachel turned on her heel, her curls swinging. She flicked up the hood of her cloak. "I'm going for a walk," she said icily, before marching out of the room.

Morpheus took one step after her, but stopped. Guy looked up from where he'd been picking at a thread in his tunic. "I doubt that going after her will do you much good, at the moment," he said.

Morpheus's face reddened when he looked at Guy. "Go to Tartarus," he snapped, before sweeping into another room and slamming the door shut behind him. The force from the slamming door put out the candle beside it, and Will occupied himself by watching the smoke wisp up towards the ceiling.

.   .   .   .   .

The streets of Athens were devoid of any people. Rachel walked alone, her head down, still covered by her red cowl. Tears slid down her cheeks as she recollected, for what was probably the fifth time, her conversation with Ewan. Or … well, it hadn't been much of a conversation. More like an argument. But every bit of frustration she'd felt towards him in five years had exploded out like magma from a volcano. How could he be so selfish? How could he not understand how his decision had affected her?

She didn't even know what to call him anymore. Ewan? Morpheus? Just who was he? She didn't know. Neither did she really want to think about it, at the moment. She didn't want to think about much of anything, to be honest. She was just tired of everything. Tired of The Story, tired of thinking, tired of trying to decide what was best for everybody. Maybe that was why Ewan had chosen to do what he did. But it was no excuse for abandoning his little sister after promising never to do so.

Rachel was so wrapped up in her own thoughts, she didn't hear the man approaching her from behind until he spoke. "Is something amiss?"

The sly, almost cold voice made Rachel stop walking and turn to face him. By the light of the torches lining the streets, she saw a man with a cold, cruel face, stony black eyes, and graying blond hair. Like most people, he dwarfed Rachel. He went on, his voice smooth as ice, "You seem troubled."

He put Rachel in mind of some kind of a sleazy businessman or something. Even his clothes—a black shirt and breeches—were different from those of Greece. Too perfect. Not like the chitons the other inhabitants wore. "I'm sulking," she admitted, while still watching him cautiously. "Who are you?"

The man spread his hands with a smile, showing just how thin and bloodless his lips actually were. "I am known by many names, Rachel Andric." The use of Rachel's name put her on edge, and she took a step back, watching him. "But you will probably know me best by the name of Hades, Lord of the Underworld, King of the dead."

Instinctively, Rachel took another step back, her eyes going wide. "You—you're Hades?" she said, her hand instinctively falling to the pommel of her blade.

"Ahh, you don't need to fear me, lovely one," Hades said. "It's Morpheus, your brother, who annoys me."

"He ... annoys you?" Rachel asked tentatively.

"Well ..." Hades scratched his chin, as if deep in thought. "Perhaps 'annoy' is too light a word. 'Vex' is more appropriate."

Rachel just stared at him, unable to think of a response. Hades wasn't finished yet, though. "You see, your brother has the hairbrained idea that we gods shouldn't be, well, *gods*. I tried to kill him earlier, but he escaped with his life, unfortunately. Your brother is a sly one, my dear."

"So ... you tried to kill my brother," Rachel said, staring at him. "And you're telling me this—*why*?"

"To tell you that it's not you I hate," Hades explained. The only word that could describe him was *amiable*. "It's your brother, of course. But then, his annoying behavior might have rubbed off on you, since you are his sister. Are you annoying?"

Rachel huffed. "Not nearly as annoying as he is."

"It would be very difficult to achieve that, my dear," Hades said, reaching forward. Although Rachel flinched, he only took ahold of one of her curls and tugged on it. "And because I find you a most charming young woman, allow me to warn you. Someone wants that pretty blonde head of yours."

"I don't suppose you mean my hair," Rachel said, trying to gain the upper hand.

Hades threw back his head and guffawed. "No, I don't mean your hair, you spunky girl!" he said. "How I so hate to do this to you ... you have my undying respect. And for the god of the dead, that's saying something. However, although you have my respect, your brother doesn't. So ... I'm sorry."

Rachel drew her sword instinctively, lunging forward. Before she could reach Hades, though, the ground seemed to split open, and two figures rose out of it. "Skeletons?" she complained, coming to an abrupt halt. "How is that fair?"

The two in front of her raised weapons, rusted swords that still looked deadly. Maybe taking a walk hadn't been her best idea, but Ewan had failed to warn her that the god of the dead wanted him ... well, dead.

Unfortunately, Hades's skeletons in front of her distracted her from the real threat of two more behind her. One grabbed her arms, jerking them behind her with surprising strength. The other placed a sword at her side, threatening without piercing skin. Hades patted Rachel's cheek cheerfully. "Don't you worry, my dear. I won't hurt you. As for my employer, that's another matter. Although, your brother's cooperation will have a good deal to do with your chances of survival ..."

"I'm not afraid of you," Rachel said, her sword on the ground. The skeleton had ripped it from her grasp.

"Well, we'll see about that," Hades answered. "I hope you enjoy the Underworld."

The ground split open beneath her, and the last thing she remembered was falling, everything around her completely black as she fell.

Chapter 20: To the Underworld

A few hours had passed without Rachel returning from her "walk". Red was slightly concerned over the Guardian's absence, but evidently the others weren't. Guy was lying on his back on one of the beds, his hands locked behind his head, while Will was curled up on his side, fast asleep. Morpheus had yet to emerge from his room after his argument with her. Red sat beside the bed, idly flipping through the one book she had brought from her home—*Robin Hood and the Merry Men*.

Guy glanced over at Red, but he didn't say anything. She continued watching him even after he'd looked away. Any fool—aside from Will, who wasn't the most observant of people—could see that the knight felt something for Rachel, even if he himself wasn't sure what it was. Red wasn't entirely certain that was a good thing. Like her uncle, she knew what had to happen when Rachel would eliminate the intruder from The Story—it would restart and return to its normal course of events.

And when it did that, Red, Guy, and Will wouldn't even remember that Rachel had ever existed.

Red stared at a picture in the book of Little John and Robin Hood fighting on a bridge, though her mind was far from that. It dwelled more on the fact that she wouldn't be living with her uncle anymore, when The Story returned to its natural course. Part of her ached when she thought about that. She loved Uncle Charles, and she had long since come to terms with the fact that her family was gone. He was the only family she really felt she had anymore.

Red closed the book and laid it on the floor next to her. She decided to get some rest where she could, and closed her eyes to sleep.

Of course, the instant she did so, the door to the temple slammed open, startling her. That was nothing compared to Will; the poor boy was shocked awake and rolled out of bed, hitting the floor with a *thud*. Guy shot to his feet as a man sprinted into the room, completely ignoring the three already present that he had run past.

They just stared at him as he hurried to Morpheus's door and started pounding on it, yelling in Greek. Red and Guy exchanged puzzled looks as Will stared at the man from the floor. "What's going on?" the outlaw asked blearily.

Red shrugged. "I believe we shall soon find out," she answered.

The door opened, and Morpheus spoke to the man in rapid-fire Greek. The conversation sent Red's head spinning, since she couldn't make out a single word of it. It lasted for less than a minute, and with a wave of his hand, Morpheus dismissed the messenger. Still without looking at Morpheus's guests, the man bowed and ran back out.

"What is happening?" Red demanded the instant the man was gone.

To Red's eternal annoyance, Morpheus didn't deign her question with a response. Instead, he turned on his heel and went back into his room. Fortunately—for him, as Red planned to hit him on the head with her club if he refused to answer her again—he emerged only moments later with a sword in his hand. He tossed the sheathed weapon to Guy, who caught it with ease. "We're leaving," Morpheus said.

"Leaving?" Red repeated. "And going where?"

"Rachel's been kidnapped," Morpheus answered abruptly. "By Hades. We have to go to the Underworld to save her. I swear by Zeus's beard—that man has crossed me for the *last* time!"

"The Underworld?" Will scratched his head. "What's that?"

"The land of the dead," Morpheus said. He marched past them, and Red caught a glimpse of a blade sheathed on his back as he walked by. "And we're going right to its master."

The other three followed along behind him, unable to keep up with the long, purposeful strides. The messenger had evidently woken all the people sleeping in the temple, and they scrambled up to a kneeling position, bowing and scraping as Morpheus swept past without even a backwards glance. As they emerged into the pitch-black streets of Athens, Red caught a glimpse of Will's frown in the light of a torch.

She sighed unobtrusively. Now was not the time to be nitpicking other people's religions; they had more important things to worry about. Will caught the look she was giving him and looked away. Guy remained stony-faced as he tramped after Morpheus. The explanation concerning what had happened to Rachel had been unsatisfying, to say the least.

However, apparently it was greatly concerning to Morpheus, judging from the way he was walking. The speed with which he was moving threatened to leave them all far behind him, but Red refused to allow herself that shame and followed as best she could.

With the speed that Morpheus was setting, they left Athens in a matter of minutes and made their way out to the grassy area beyond. Once the walls of the city were several hundred feet away, Morpheus stopped and heaved a sigh. Then he raised his eyes and shouted, "Hermes! I need you!"

For several moments, there was no response. Then a glaring-white door materialized in front of them, and a man stepped through. Unlike Morpheus, he wore the usual chiton

168

of a Greek person, and his sandals had *wings* on them. Red saw Will staring at the peculiar sandals, and she had to conceal a smile. The man, who must have been Hermes, looked exhausted. "Come on, Morpheus," he complained, his voice higher-pitched than Morpheus's by quite a bit. "It's late. Couldn't this, I don't know, wait until morning?"

"I would've waited if it wasn't an *emergency*," Morpheus replied, brushing aside the other man's complaint. "Hades has kidnapped my sister and taken her to the Underworld. One of my messengers came and told me. I don't even want to *think* about what he could do to her to get at me."

"Ahh, true," Hermes said, running a hand through his sandy-colored hair. A moment later, he rolled his umber eyes. "Honestly, though, can't he be a little more *creative*? Kidnapping a girl and taking her to the Underworld? It's Persephone all over again!"

"Except he took Persephone to the Underworld because he loved her," Morpheus said, with a tone of voice that indicated he had only the tiniest amount of patience remaining. "Hades certainly *doesn't* love Rachel. Or me, for that matter, which probably has more of an effect on it."

"True, true," Hermes agreed. "I suppose you want me to send you to the Underworld? Try to be more careful. Remember what happened *last* time you went?"

Morpheus's face twitched. "Did you really have to remind me?"

"Just a friendly warning from a friend," Hermes said. "And I am *not* going with you. Just so you know."

"Oh, I know," Morpheus said. "Can you send us there now? Time is of the essence."

Hermes nodded, snapping his fingers. Another door of light appeared, but this one was tinged with shadows around the border. "Don't die, Morph," he said. "If you died, I wouldn't be able to talk to anybody else. After all, you're the only one who's not obsessed with one thing or another."

"Oh, I'm obsessed," Morpheus said with grim humor, and Red was sure that he looked right at Guy. The knight seemed aware of that, for his face reddened and he hastily looked away. Will was still staring at the sandals. "I just don't blab about it every second like the other gods do. Thanks, Hermes. I owe you."

Hermes swept a bow. "That's what friends are for—sending other friends to the land of the dead," he replied. "Goodbye, Morph." His wings flapped once before he stepped backwards, shimmered for a moment, and disappeared.

Red glanced over at Will, whose face was getting paler and paler with every passing second. She nudged him with her arm, and he managed to smile a little at her. Morpheus, who had been staring at the spot where Hermes had disappeared, tore his attention away, back to the others. "Is everyone ready?" he asked, his voice hard. "The Underworld isn't for the faint of heart." His gaze lingered on Guy hatefully. Red bit down on her lip. Why did he hate the man so much?

"I'm ready," Will said, looking up and nodding slowly. Red and Guy mirrored his movement but didn't say anything.

Morpheus took a deep breath. "Then let's go."

.   .   .   .   .

When the small group stepped through the door, they found themselves on the shore of a creepy lake. Red looked around as the door disappeared from behind them. The Underworld seemed lit by an odd, eerie green light that seemed to make all her companions look as if they were dead as well. Judging from the expression on Will's expressive face, he found the whole situation to be extremely nerve-wracking.

The waves lapped at the black shore, crunchy sand that cracked under Red's feet. The roof of the cavern was craggy and made of that same black stone. A dock stretched out over the river, and a rickety boat rocked gently on the waves. Impulsively, Red started making her way towards it, but Morpheus grabbed her arm. "Wait," he said. "You touch that water and you'll be trapped in it as a spirit for all eternity. It's the River Styx."

"You mean, until The Story restarts?" Red asked.

Morpheus shook his head. "I wish. It's forever. Irreversible. Trust me, you're best bet is to stay away from the river."

Red frowned. "But there is no other path available to us," she said.

Will was turning a light shade of green. "I've never been on a boat before," he said, his voice tight.

"Eh, it's not so bad as all that," Morpheus replied. "Don't you worry a bit about it. It's not like Hades has sunk the boat with me and Hermes in it before."

Guy's lips twitched. "Why do I get the feeling you're being sarcastic?" he said.

Morpheus raised his eyebrows. "Because I am. Come on. Hades wouldn't have gone to all the trouble of letting one of my men see him kidnap Rachel if he wanted to kill us off the bat." He marched down the slope of black sand to the rickety dock, and the others reluctantly followed him, Red most reluctantly of all. His story of the River Styx hadn't exactly made her feel confident about it.

As they reached the boat, a large group of bats flew overhead, making all four of them duck. The ugly creatures gathered on the boat and formed the black cloak of a figure, holding out a startling-white boney hand towards them, palm-up. The boat stilled its rock when the figure appeared in it.

Red dared to look under the figure's hood, and she instinctively grabbed Will's arm when she saw the creature's face—a skeleton, grinning blankly at them. "That is unholy," Will gasped.

Morpheus ignored them, marching to the end of the dock. He dug into his pocket and produced a golden coin, laying it in the skeleton's palm. The skeleton spoke, his voice seeming to come from around them, rather than from his mouth. "Morpheus, god of sleep and dreams. This really is becoming a bad habit with you, isn't it?"

"Not my fault, Charon," Morpheus said, sighing. "Hades keeps calling me. I don't have enough gold for all my passengers; surely you know me well enough for one to count?"

If the skeleton's expression could have changed, Red sensed that it would have been approving. "Yes, Lord Morpheus, I believe an exception could be made for a regular like you. You are free to pass. The boat shall guide you. Fear not, mortals. The boat shall not disappoint you."

"Thank you, Charon," Morpheus replied, smiling just the tiniest bit. Red noticed how much more handsome his face became when he relaxed it. Mentally, she slapped herself. What kind of a thought was that?

Charon disappeared into yet another flock of bats, which made Red cringe. Rodents. Ugh, she hated them. Her train of thought was disrupted once more by Morpheus hopping into the boat. The ease with which he moved failed to reassure Red, and she made her way to the end of the dock nervously. Her ankle ached, though there was no outward sign of any injury. Morpheus turned and grabbed her around the waist, lifting her into the boat, and for some ridiculous reason,

172

instead of hitting him in the head with her club, she just blushed.

Will gave a perceptible swallow before gingerly climbing in behind Red. Then he and Morpheus held the boat steady for Guy as the knight eased himself in, trying to rock it as little as possible. Once all four of them had fit in the admittedly-small boat, Morpheus cut the rotting rope with his blade, and the boat slid off, in the river.

Red huddled next to Will, holding her stomach. As they got further down the river, she could hear peculiar sounds, like weeping, and screams. She didn't dare look over at the green, swirling water; her stomach was ill at ease enough already. Will, however, seemed to have made that mistake and was now turning an even darker shade of green.

Guy remained at the prow of the boat, staring down. The only outward sign of his nerves was that he continually slid his blade in and out of its sheath. He kept glancing at Morpheus, who was staring at the river. Red thought she detected a trace of tears in his eyes that seemed to make him that much more human. "Are you well?" she asked him softly.

Morpheus looked up at her and managed a smile. "Good enough. I'll feel a lot better when we reach dry land," he said. "Although I doubt I'll ever feel 'well' in the Underworld. The whole place creeps me out."

Will reached into his quiver, pulling out an arrow. He started tapping it with his finger, mostly watching Morpheus. "Have you been here a lot?" he asked.

"Quite a bit," Morpheus said. "Hades doesn't like me. He attacked me just this morning." He tugged his cloak and shirt aside, revealing a large burn on his shoulder. "Luckily, I managed to escape from him, but this is a hundred times worse than anything he could do to me." He rubbed his face.

"I've missed Rachel more than I can say. I'm just sorry that our reunion was ruined by an argument."

"We'll get her back," Will assured him. "I know we will."

"You're optimistic, aren't you?" Morpheus said. "I hope you're right, Will. Because if you're not, then ... I don't know what we'll do for The Story."

Guy looked up. "You don't have to think about that. Surely we can fight this Hades."

"Possibly." Morpheus shrugged. "The fact remains, if he's got any allies, we're doomed. I should know."

"We'll find out," Red answered.

Minutes later, the boat turned off onto a side route, and Morpheus looked significantly more nervous. "We've moved to the River Lethe," he said, leaning over the side somewhat and frowning. "One drop of water from this river, and your mind will be as fresh as a newborn baby's. You'll lose all your memories and every sense of the person you used to be."

"I ... see ..." Will looked even more unnerved, if that was even possible. "It seems that the Underworld's not the best place to take a swim, then."

"It would seem not," Red agreed. "Where will this vessel land?"

"Wherever Hades wants it to, unfortunately," Morpheus said. "So we may as well get comfortable. We're not in charge of this. Whether I like it or not, Hades is in charge."

"*Bien*," Red muttered sarcastically, curling up more. She wished she hadn't eaten anything before they'd left her Story. It was all tumbling around in her stomach.

Without warning, the boat rammed into the shore, nearly dislodging Guy from his position at the prow. Once it became apparent that the boat wouldn't be moving anymore,

Morpheus swung his long legs over the side and hopped onto dry land. The others, after hesitating, followed him.

The shore was only a small island, occupied only by Hades and the bound figure of Rachel Andric, standing beside him. The Lord of the Underworld stood two heads taller than the slim Guardian, and his arrogant face tightened into a smile when he saw them. "Good day, Morpheus," he said. "Come closer, and leave your weapons there, unless you want the lovely blonde girl to take a swim in the River Lethe."

Will laid an arrow on his bowstring, but Morpheus put a restraining hand on his bow. "Save shooting for a last resort," he warned him quietly. "He'll push Rachel in, if he thinks it'll serve his purpose." Then he dropped his sword to the ground before walking towards Hades. "Don't touch her, Hades. I'm coming."

"I don't want to go up there unarmed," Guy muttered, but he unsheathed his sword and dropped it to the sand. Will followed suit, but Red kept her club concealed under her cloak. It was a gamble, but she didn't think that Hades would push Rachel in unless as a last resort.

They all stopped several feet from Hades and his hostage. Rachel raised her eyes to them, unable to speak due to the gag wrapped around her mouth. To Red's surprise, she saw that the Guardian looked terrified. She had never looked quite so scared as she did in that moment.

Morpheus stiffened, his eyes fixed on his sister's face. "Rach," he said. She looked away, pain in her expression. Then he turned back to Hades. "Let her go, you monster. There's no need to keep her hostage anymore."

"Her? A hostage?" Hades laughed, and Red's hand crept towards her club at his tone of voice. Something wasn't quite right ... "She's not the hostage, Morpheus. They are."

Without warning, the sand beneath them parted, revealing skeletal hands. Before Red could even react to that, the hands grasped the trio, hauling themselves out of the sand and pulling their prisoners back. A sword pressed against Red's neck, and a glance showed her two friends to be in similar situations. Will was making choking noises in the back of his throat, while Guy kept his eyes squeezed shut.

Rachel cried out, the sound muffled by her gag. Morpheus swung to face them, his face going white. He turned back to Hades, reaching for his back sheath, but his sword was on the sand, near the water.

Hades laughed as if it was all a big game. "So tell me, Morpheus—is this your weakness? It's always been your friends, hasn't it? You need to learn that having friends is a detriment to you. They make you weak. And weakness leads to your downfall. Physically, I have orders not to injure her—" He indicated Rachel, who couldn't take her eyes off the hostages—"but nobody has told me I can't hurt *them*."

As if to prove his point, the swords dug in a little more, drawing blood. Red hissed, whitening her knuckles on her club, but she couldn't try anything, not while the other two were still being held prisoner. And she knew that Hades would push Rachel into the water if he was backed against a wall. Oddly enough, although she hardly knew any of them, she couldn't bear the thought of abandoning any of them to their fate.

Morpheus found his voice. "Stop this!" he said. He didn't shout, but his tone left no doubt as to his determination—and his desperation. "Leave them be. We can … we can make some kind of a deal."

Judging from the triumphant light on Hades's face, that was exactly what he'd been pushing for the entire time. That fact made Red very, very nervous. "Oh, yes," he said,

176

rubbing his hands together. Rachel was scowling at her brother. "A deal could be *very* interesting, god of sleep and dreams. Just what kind do you have in mind?"

Morpheus looked at Red briefly before turning his gaze back to Rachel. She desperately shook her head from side to side, her face cast in the ghastly light of the Underworld. Hades interrupted Morpheus before he could say anything. "Oh, and mind you, it has to be *quite* the deal. My employer is most keen on having them." He pointed at Rachel and Will.

When Morpheus's shoulders slumped, Red's heart fell. *Don't do anything stupid,* she thought desperately. "Fine," Morpheus said, stepping one foot forward, towards Hades and Rachel. "I swear this oath on the River Styx."

"Don't do anything foolish," Guy snapped, his voice hoarse. "Don't be a fool!"

Morpheus ignored him, his fists clenched. "I swear on the River Styx that if you let Rachel, Guy of Gisborne, Will Scarlet, and Red Riding Hood return to the surface *unharmed,* the next time The Story restarts, I will undergo Final Death. Do you agree to that deal?"

Rachel screamed through her gag, struggling to be freed from her bonds. Hades shoved her to the ground. "But waiting for The Story to restart will take such a dreadfully long time," Hades complained.

"Rachel is on a quest to restart The Story and write the intruder out," Morpheus said calmly. "Even if she fails, the intruder will likely do the same thing. So either way, I'll be dead in less than a few weeks, if even. Do we have a deal, Hades?"

"Fool," Red whispered, biting down on her lip hard. Only pure insanity would lead a man to make such a foolish deal!

Hades thought about it for only another few moments before his face split into a devilish grin. "I accept the terms of your deal!" he said, and snapped his fingers. The skeletons dissolved, freeing their prisoners. Rachel's bindings vanished, and, off-balance, she could do nothing as Hades grabbed her arm.

"Hades ..." Morpheus reached forward, anxiety sprouting up in his features. "Let her go. We had a deal."

"I'm aware," Hades said. "But your deal involved physical harm ... not mental." He swung around to hurl the girl into the river. At the same time, the sand shifted beneath Will, sending the boy backwards.

Guy had already been moving forward before Hades had said a word. He sprinted towards them, kicking up sand as he ran. Just as Hades released Rachel, intending to send her flying into the River Styx, Guy grabbed her arm, jerking her to safety. Rachel collapsed against him, sobbing helplessly.

Red swung around when she heard Will cry out. The boy was falling backwards, the sand heaving beneath him. "Will!" she yelled, grabbing at his shirt in an effort to catch him. He was close, too close, to the water.

For a moment, the tactic worked and she tried to pull him away from the water. But the shirt didn't hold, and it tore in her grasp. Red could only watch in horror as Will's arms pinwheeled, desperately, trying to hold his balance when it was already impossible.

Then he tipped backwards, falling into the River Lethe with a loud splash.

Chapter 21: Memories

When Rachel heard Red and Will cry out, she broke free from Guy's grasp and stared in horror. Red stood on the shore, backing away from the water, which was ... utterly still. Ewan ran to Red, pulling her back. "Stay away!" he ordered. "Keep back. Don't touch him!"

Rachel swung on Hades, hoping to punch him in the face, but the treacherous god had already disappeared. Cursing to herself, she ran to where Ewan and Red were, staring at the eerily green water of the Lethe. Guy followed silently, muttering something under his breath. Terror coursed through Rachel as she stared at the water. What if he'd drowned? What if he'd forgotten *everything*?

A pale hand emerged from the water, narrowly avoiding splashing them all. Will's fingers grasped at the sand, trying to find some leverage to pull himself out. If his grasp was to slip, then he would end up back in the water, and ... what if he drowned?

Rachel reacted purely out of instinct. Paying no attention to Ewan's shout of, "NO!" she lunged forward and grabbed Will's wrist before he could fall back into the water. Immediately, she felt drops of water beneath her fingers, and her vision tunneled.

·   ·   ·   ·   ·

I paced along the side of the cliff, watching the waves crash against our island. I ignored how the wind tossed my hair into my face, blinding me with tears that weren't just from the impact. My nightgown swept around me, whipping around. Lightning lit the sky, splitting it up like a chasm. "Ewan," I whispered, my voice lost in the wind and thunder. "Where are you?"

As if in answer to my question, I felt my stomach give a lurch as The Story Book "opened" and released someone. For some reason, I didn't move from my spot to meet Ewan. Let him come to me first. I knew what he'd been planning. I could only hope that he hadn't succeeded.

Only a few seconds later, I heard the sound of running feet coming up behind me, over the sound of the storm. Still, my face remained set on the sea, not turning around. "Rach! Rachel!" Ewan was behind me, and I did turn around now, to face him. He was grinning from ear to ear, but he looked terrible. A slash was across his forehead, his Greek chiton was ripped and bloodied, and he was covered in sand, but he'd never looked happier. A strange sinking sensation settled in my stomach. "I did it, Rachel!" he added, scooping me up in his arms and swinging me around.

I grabbed his arms, squirming until he put me down. "What did you do?" I said, hoping against hope that it wasn't what I thought it was. "Ewan, what in the world did you do?"

He hugged me against my will. "I changed it," he said. "I changed The Story! I saved the life of Achilles. Isn't that fantastic?"

With a good deal of struggling, I managed to squirm free from my brother's grasp. "Ewan, what have you done?" My voice was shrill, tight. I had known for some time what he'd planned to do, but my fervent prayers that he wouldn't follow through with it had always been answered. Until now ...

A lump formed in my throat as Ewan ignored my distress and grabbed my shoulders, shaking me enthusiastically. "I saved him, Rach," he said, pulling me into another hug. "If I can save one life, I can save more, I know I can! I rescued Achilles from Paris's arrow!"

Fear rushed through me as his words truly dawned in my mind. Furious, I slapped him across the face as hard as I could. The sting of my palm failed to halt my ire. "Are you stupid?" I yelled at him. "Are you intent on leaving me like our parents did? You know what's going to happen to you! You ... you're going to be ..." My voice caught, because I knew what was going to happen.

Drunk on his victory, Ewan either didn't know or didn't care. "I made it back here, didn't I?" he boasted, brushing his black hair out of his face and smiling widely. "I'm safe. They can't possibly get to me here." Even as he spoke, I could see his form begin to change, deteriorate.

And then it did deteriorate, dissolving into a fine black powder. Too late, I tried to grab my brother's arm, only for it to become dust in my grasp. As I pulled my hand back, staring at it in horror, the black powder that was my brother morphed into a single cloud before blowing back on the path. In its place was a fluttering piece of paper. Without even thinking, I grabbed the paper before running after the dust, as if I could do something about it.

The chase took me into the house, up the stairs, and into the room holding The Story. It was there that I saw the powder land on the cover and seep into the pages. Without even realizing it, I was crying, staring at The Story Book. The paper crinkled under the power of my grasp. The only thing that drew me out of my stupor was when the edge of it slipped and dug into my hand as a papercut.

As if in a daze, I opened the letter and read it in the gloomy light of the room.
Rachel Andric:
Your brother, Ewan Andric, has been tried and found guilty of breaking the rules of a Guardian by trying to save The Story and saving Achilles's life. Punishment has been enacted and your

brother has been stripped of his role as a Guardian and written into The Story. We apologize for any inconvenience.

Although the letter was unsigned, I knew it was from the Guardians, without a doubt. Furious, grieving, confused, and sleep-deprived from worry, I clenched the letter in my fist, ignorant of the blood seeping down my palm. Then, as realization fully dawned on me, I fell to my knees, sobbing.

The Story had restarted, and my brother was now a part of it.

Permanently.

·   ·   ·   ·   ·

Pulling herself out of her memory, Rachel blinked to find that she was still in the Underworld. With a yank, she dragged Will free of the water, and both of them collapsed backwards, gasping for air for two completely different reasons. The others stood in a circle, not close enough that the water would splash on them.

Ewan knelt beside Rachel, his face tight with worry. "Rach!" he said. "Are you alright? Do you remember me?"

Rachel blinked at him, confused at seeing him outside of that memory. That horrible, horrible memory. "Of course I remember you," she said, a little waspishly.

Ewan was taken aback by her cold response. "Oh, I, uh ... that's good."

Red was watching the soaking-wet Will, who was currently coughing up Lethe water onto the sand. "And Will?" she asked. "Do you remember us?"

Will rubbed the back of his hand over his mouth with a look of disgust. "Ugh, that felt horrible," he muttered before looking up at Red. "Of course I do. Why wouldn't I?"

"It's the River Lethe?" Guy said, raising his eyebrows. "That's supposed to wipe your memories if you even touch it?"

Will stared at the drops of water covering him. "Really?" he said. "I think it's broken, then."

Ewan ignored him, putting his hand on Rachel's shoulder. "Rach, are you *sure* you're okay?" he asked worriedly.

Rachel jerked away from him. "Yes. I'm fine!" she said in exasperation. All her anger from that moment five years ago came rushing back to her. The entirety of her fury from her time spent alone because of his choice, her ire that he'd abandoned her for no reason, and even her anger from their conversation from before she'd been kidnapped by Hades, it all came back with an unpleasant yet satisfying desire to hurt him. "Just leave me alone, you fool."

"Rachel—" Will began, looking awkward.

Rachel was feeling even less well-disposed towards him. "You don't talk to me, either."

"I think you are being a bit unfair," Red snapped. "We did just delve into the Underworld to save your *ingrat* hide."

"I am not ungrateful!" Rachel protested, squirming uncomfortably. "You should have just left me alone!"

"I do believe that might translate into being ungrateful," Guy put in smoothly. "However, we should probably leave, before Hades changes his mind."

Ewan gave Guy a superior look. "Hades literally can't change his mind," he told him. "He swore the oath. If he broke it, he'd just end up in the River Styx. Anyway, I do agree with you—we should probably get going. I hate the Underworld."

Rachel was noticing with growing annoyance that Ewan seemed to enjoy correcting Guy. However, she did agree with his and Guy's sentiments that they needed to leave. The place just made her utterly uncomfortable. The little group followed Ewan to the beach, where a boat had surfaced once more to take them across the rivers. Ewan glared at it for a moment before climbing in.

Will did not look particularly enthusiastic, but he climbed in after, and the others followed suit. The boat rocked and creaked more than before, but they forced themselves to ignore it and set off through the Underworld, back to the sun above.

Chapter 22: Back Safely

Their trip back to Ewan's temple was uneventful and silent. Nobody spoke to anybody else. Although they had left the Underworld behind them physically, it still hung heavy over their minds; it was a horrible place that Rachel doubted she could ever forget. Even the normally-irrepressible Will was quiet, eyeing the droplets of water on his skin.

There was no sign of Hermes when they emerged once more onto the hill above Athens. Ewan grunted a little and led them down to the city, ignoring everyone else. Rachel trailed after him, keeping a safe distance between herself and Will. The last thing she wanted was to touch the water ... *again.*

Both the waters of the Lethe and Queen Mal had known that the best way to manipulate her was through her emotions. Although she disguised them with a cold attitude towards everything, she was really an emotional person. And both the river and the Queen had known and manipulated that. What was she supposed to do against someone or something that knew her every weakness?

And, to be honest, she was furious at Ewan. He had essentially abandoned her, even though he'd promised not to, and left her with nobody, on an island in the middle of nowhere, with faulty magical electricity. That sounded like a great older brother, didn't it? She hated him for what he'd done to her, yet she loved him more than she loved anything else in the world. It was all just too complicated.

The entirety of Rachel's muddled emotions had come rushing back when she'd come into contact with the soaked Will, and she knew he'd seen them as well. Whether he understood them was another matter entirely, but it was bad enough that he'd been a second witness to them. Added to that was his obvious confusion at how he had retained his memories after falling into the river itself. Ewan had probably given them all sorts of dire warnings about it.

That was another thing. The way everyone called him Morpheus, like he wasn't Rachel's brother. Like he wasn't Ewan. And was he anymore? Who knew how many times The Story had restarted since Ewan had been written in? How many different lives he'd lived? Had he fallen in love? Morpheus had different parents than Ewan did. Had he replaced their family? Was that why he'd gone into The Story? To replace the parents he'd lost?

Adding to her confusion were the others. First of all, they'd risk their lives by going to the Underworld in the first place. She knew they all wanted to protect The Story for their own reasons, but she wondered if that was the only reason they'd come to save her. If it wasn't because of The Story, then what was it? Did they really just ... like her? She didn't know.

They entered the city, but Rachel was still lost in thought. The sun was now shining overhead, probably around nine in the morning. They had been in the Underworld overnight, which was a creepy thought, considering that it hadn't felt like that long. She tried to ignore the feeling inside of her—anger, fury, grief—and just kept walking. That was all she could do. Just keep putting one foot forward, and follow with the other. All she wanted was to crash on a bed and fall asleep. To not think about anything anymore.

The group made their way back to Ewan's temple, which was empty after the time of sleeping had come to an end. Rachel's brother then went into a side room, tossed Will some clothes, and told him to burn the ones he was wearing, as well as the towel he was given to dry off. The boy disappeared into the opposing room to change and do as he was told.

While he did that and Ewan went into the kitchen to fix them all something to eat, Red and Guy stretched out on the beds and fell asleep. Rachel watched them for a while, until Will emerged. Then she motioned for him to follow her; the two went outside and sat on the steps of the temple, watching the Greek crowds hurry by.

For a few minutes, the two of them sat in silence. Finally, Will looked down at his hands, very carefully avoiding Rachel's gaze, and mumbled, "I'm sorry for prying into your memories like that."

"Prying?" Rachel repeated, wondering how this conversation would go. Then she sighed. It was definitely time for her to let go of pushing people away. "You weren't prying, Will. It's my own fault for grabbing you when Ewan warned me repeatedly not to. I just wasn't thinking, so the blame's all on my shoulders. Really, don't worry about it. It's okay."

Judging from the way Will was kneading his hands together, he *was* worried about it. "I ... I can't stop thinking," he admitted softly. "I'm ... I'm not normal, Rachel. I'm the only one who doesn't remember his Story, the only one who can maintain his memories after touching the River Lethe. I have no side-effects from it at all! I'm fine! Completely fine, and I shouldn't be."

"Shouldn't you be happy about that?" Rachel said, feigning indifference. She didn't want him to know just how strange that actually was.

Will glared half-jokingly at her. "Oh, you know what I mean," he said.

She shrugged. "Okay, yes, I do know what you mean, but it's *fine*, Will. We'll figure it all out. Chances are, you're just one of the little bumps that occurs in The Story. Easily fixed. It's what the Guardians are supposed to do, after all."

Instead of making him smile, Rachel's words made his shoulders slump. "So all I am to you is a 'little bump'?" he asked.

Rachel grimaced. "No, Will. You know I don't think that. You ... you're my friend. I think."

The time she *wasn't* trying to make him laugh, he did. "That doesn't sound very positive," he commented, chuckling.

Feeling uncomfortable, Rachel spread her hands. "I ... it's just, well, I don't really know what having a friend's like. Even when I had my family, it was still just us. So ... you'll have to excuse me if I seem a little ... odd."

Will laughed again. "Alright, you're excused, Milady Andric," he said. "Besides, you saved my life. I think that qualifies you as my friend."

Rachel smiled slightly. "As long as you didn't mind me calling you a 'little bump'," she answered.

Will snorted. "Rachel, have you ever fixed any of these so-called 'little bumps'?" he asked. "I mean, you are a Guardian, so ..."

Rachel picked at the bottom of her red cloak. "No. I've never even been into The Story before now." *Thanks to Ewan, this is really the first heart-to-heart chat I've had with anyone in about forever too.* She fought down more bitterness.

"Ah." Will, perhaps wisely, chose not to pursue that particular subject. Instead, he shook his head slightly. "Seems like I've got a target on my back. If something is going to happen to one of us, seems like it's going to happen to me."

"I got kidnapped by Hades, hit over the head by your uncle, and cursed by Mal," Rachel reminded him.

Will shrugged. "Well, technically we *all* got kidnapped by Hades. I also almost got hung, as well as getting clawed by the Wolf, and then I got thrown into the River Lethe."

Rachel laughed. "You have a point," she said.

188

"I know I do!" Will said. "And people like to actually stick that point into me!"

The two of them chuckled over that for a few minutes before lapsing into a companionable silence. It lasted for a few minutes, until Will broke it again. "You've been doing well, Rachel."

She turned to look at him incredulously. "Doing well?" she repeated, her eyebrows shooting up. "I've been stumbling around, basically lost, with almost no idea of what to do. We were just going over the list of disasters that have been inflicted upon me. How is that 'doing well'?"

Will shrugged. "We're not dead yet," he said. "Seriously, though, we came to rescue you because we believe in you, Rachel. The Story is in your hands, and I believe they're in capable hands. Maybe I don't really understand the concept of The Story, or how it works, but I know enough about it to realize that this intruder fellow is threatening many people's lives. We rely on you, Rachel. Because you have what the intruder and the Guardians are both lacking—kindness."

Rachel looked at him askance. "What do you mean? The Guardians lack in kindness?" she asked. "No ... I'm afraid not. They have rules that need to be followed, Will, and Ewan broke them. I don't blame them for what they did. It was his own fault for breaking their rules."

"I saw that whole scene from your eyes," Will reminded her. "I know how you felt when that happened. Inside, you really wanted Morpheus—erm, Ewan—to succeed. Deep down within you, you feel the same way that he does. That the people of The Story deserve a better life. That they shouldn't have to experience the same things every Story cycle. That they should be free to make their own choices. You hide that better than Ewan did; you know what fate will

189

be awaiting you if you choose the same path that he did. A simple and stupid stand that would just result in you getting punished. But deep down inside, you want the same thing Ewan does—to get a chance to rewrite The Story."

For several seconds, Rachel stared at him, unable to come up with a decent response. Then she stood, her cloak whipping around her in annoyance. "Okay, you know how you were worried that you were prying before? You're prying *now*."

"Rachel, I didn't mean—" Will stammered, surprised.

"It doesn't matter," Rachel said, though it mattered a great deal to her. "I'm going to see if dinner—"

"Breakfast," Will said, indicating the rising sun.

"Whichever!" Rachel snapped, losing her patience with the outlaw. "I'm going to go see if *breakfast* is ready."

And before he could say anything or even apologize, she'd marched back up the stairs and into the temple.

Chapter 23: The Andrics

Although Rachel marched back into the temple's inner rooms with obvious annoyance, she was relieved to discover that Red and Guy were fast asleep on two of the beds. That saved her an explanation to them, at least for now. Heaving a sigh, Rachel sat down on one herself, watching her sleeping ... friends? Could she even call them her friends, when she'd known them for only a short amount of time? They *had* gone into the Underworld to rescue her, though ...

Mostly, though, Rachel's thoughts were on her conversation with Will. He wasn't wrong, about what she wanted. The longer she'd been in The Story, the more she'd begun to realize that they didn't deserve the lot in life they'd been given. Even those who didn't die a terrible death were cursed never to be able to enjoy the "happily ever after" they received, since immediately after they got it, The Story started back from the beginning! How was that fair?

She was so lost in her own thoughts, she didn't hear Ewan come up behind her. A tap on her shoulder broke her out of her reverie, and she turned to look at her older brother quizzically. A small part of her wished he would just leave her alone, but the grief of the past five years cut off any retort she had for him.

Apparently deciding that her silence invited him to say more, Ewan indicated the door he'd just come out of with his head. "It's almost time to eat," he said softly, in an effort not to wake Red and Guy. "Can we talk?"

Rachel let him tug her to her feet and guide her to the room. She risked a backward glance and saw Guy's eyes, open and watching them go, just before the door swung shut behind them. Once in the kitchen, she became aware of a mouthwatering scent—eggs cooking. Ewan made his way through the dim kitchen, illuminated only by the light of the fire, and looked in the pot. "Not quite done," he said, mostly to himself, before turning back to Rachel. "It's been a while since we've been alone together, hasn't it?"

Rachel stared at the floor, her face red. "And whose fault is that?" she answered, some of her earlier anger rising again.

"Mine, I suppose," Ewan admitted. "Though we can kind of blame the Guardians too, can't we? Since they instituted the rules that I subsequently broke."

Rachel huffed. "That would be like blaming the government for a thief going to prison," she retorted. "They instilled the laws to protect people."

"Themselves," Ewan said. "That's all they're trying to protect. Their own arrogant egos. It's never been about *us*, it's always been about them."

"I am one of them," Rachel replied. "You were too. Until you broke their rules."

Ewan sighed. "Can we move past that for about ten minutes? Please? I just want to talk to you for a few minutes."

For a minute, Rachel considered refusing him, just to spite him for what he'd done to her. But her desire to speak to him after so long overcame that idea, and she relaxed slightly, allowing him to pull her over to two chairs. "Fine." She sat down, and he settled in across from her, leaning forward and folding his hands together.

Once they were seated, the two siblings just kind of stared at each other for a few seconds. Ewan clasped and unclasped his hands several times before finally raising his eyes to Rachel. "I'm sorry," he said finally.

"What could you possibly have to be sorry for?" Rachel answered with heavy sarcasm. "You only left me alone for five years, and then, when I finally get reunited with you,

you make a deal that will *kill* you, separating us forever. That's absolutely nothing you should be sorry for." At the end, her voice broke, and she had to turn her face away so he wouldn't see the tears trickling down her cheeks.

He did see them, though, and put his hand forward, brushing them away with his hand. His fingers were as cold as ice. "I am sorry, for all of those. The most difficult choice I made in my life was my decision of whether to be with you and feel as if I was doing something wrong, or follow my conscience and leave you behind. I would have thought that you'd return to America every now and again, like when our parents took us there when we were young."

"What would be there for me?" Rachel questioned him bitterly. "Memories, of what used to be? Besides, I can't drive a boat. I was trapped on that island for five years, with no human contact. Don't you know how much that can drive a person crazy? All I had were the memories in my mind. Ghosts, haunting my every move."

Grief seemed to be battling with something else on Ewan's face—something unreadable. "I missed you."

"Not as much as I missed you. Every day, every night," Rachel admitted, her voice barely more than a whisper. She stared down at her lap and her folded hands.

For a moment, she thought that Ewan was going to start crying. However, he composed his features and cleared his throat. "Apologies won't be enough to fix what I've done. But surely you can realize now why I had to do it."

"Enlighten me."

Ewan spread his hands helplessly. "I did it because I couldn't bear for people to suffer," he said. "People like Red, and Will. Even the gods I've met here—Apollo, Artemis, and Hermes ... do you know what fate awaits them at the end of The Story? In a war amongst the gods, they are all killed.

193

Even I am. Over and over. There is no such thing as a 'happy ending' for almost anyone in The Story."

"I understand that!" Rachel burst out. "But you took away any chances for *us* to have a happy ending too!"

Ewan groaned. "This is about more than just you and me!" he yelled. Rachel frowned at him, jerking her head in the direction of the door in warning for him to keep it down. He managed to tone down his volume, but only slightly. "You're being selfish."

To that, Rachel lost it. She stood up, her face turning a bright red. "Oh, am I?" she shot back. "Maybe you should think that *you* were being selfish, when you came into The Story to get written in! Maybe you should have thought of what I wanted. What I would've been willing to do, to stay with you!"

Ewan blinked, looking as if she'd slapped him. "I don't understand—"

"Of course you don't," Rachel interrupted him savagely. "Because you never want to see things my way! Because you always treated me like a delicate little flower! I would've done anything to stay with you. Even get written in with you. But you had to go off and do it alone. You left me behind." She sank back against her chair, covering her face, to hide the tears.

To her surprise, she felt his arms envelope her. "This is why I couldn't take you with me," he whispered. "Because you are a better person than I ever was, and ever will be. You deserve a better life than what the Guardians would have forced you in to. I never thought that you would just ... just be there alone, for five years."

As much as Rachel wanted to pull herself from his grasp, the hug was too comforting. It felt as if they'd never

194

left their island. "P-please," she begged. "Don't leave me. Don't leave me again."

A gentle hand stroked her hair as she buried her face in his shirt. She put her arms around him, crying, trying to figure out why. There was just too much going on. "You know I can't promise that," Ewan told her quietly. "But you know, even when I die ... I'll always be with you, watching over you. And I'll always be in your heart."

She didn't answer, beyond a sniff. Ewan kept stroking her hair. "I love you, Rach. And that's why I had to make that deal," he said. "Because if Hades had followed through with his threat and thrown you into the River Lethe, I wouldn't have been able to stand it. The sight of you, seeing me, but not knowing who I am. It would've killed me. I've already had to go through it once, with one of my closest friends. I just couldn't let that happen. And Hades wouldn't have accepted anything else."

Swallowing past a massive lump in her throat, Rachel pulled away. Her shaky hand came up and scrubbed at her cheeks, trying to wipe the tears away. "What happened to you?" she asked softly. "Why did you turn against The Story so much?"

Although the question seemed out of the blue to her, Ewan seemed to have expected it. His shoulders slumped and he sat back in his chair. "I guess it all started when Mom and Dad died," he admitted. "How much do you remember?"

Rachel shrugged miserably. "Not much," she admitted. "Just that, you know, they went off into a Story one day and they never came back. I think I might've pushed the memories away unconsciously, because really, I should've known, I was old enough ..."

Ewan shrugged. "Well, they went off into The Story, yeah. It was a routine mission, to save a young man who was

195

in danger of dying a Final Death. But—well—as you know, something went wrong. Terribly wrong."

Rachel couldn't take her eyes off her brother's face. However, without warning, he stood up, nearly tipping his chair over, and started pacing the room. She still followed him with her gaze. "When they entered The Story, the boy was much closer to death than they anticipated," he said. "In fact, his would-be murderer was seconds away from giving the fatal blow. Our father, he ... he pushed the boy out of the way, and he was stabbed instead. His murderer was stunned. He didn't even intend to kill Dad. Then Mom attacked the man. I don't really know if he intended to kill her, but he did. Guy swung the sword and she died."

The dropping of the name made Rachel's head snap up. "G-G-Guy?" she stammered, her fingers wrapping around one of her blonde curls. "You mean, Guy killed my parents?"

"*Our* parents," Ewan said absently. "And yes."

Rachel tugged on her hair so hard, it hurt. She never took her eyes off her brother's pacing form as she sat stiffly. "B-but ... why? Who was the—" She stopped. "No."

Ewan glanced over his shoulder at her before pacing some more. "You've probably guessed it."

Rachel swallowed. "Not ... Will?"

"Yes. Will." Ewan shifted uncomfortably, finally stopping his pacing. "Look, I know this is a lot for you to take in, but those two young men out there? They were key parts of our parents' deaths."

"Key?" Rachel resisted the urge to stand, and gripped the sides of her chair, as if to keep her from toppling off. "But—it sounds like it wasn't intentional."

"What do you mean?" Ewan asked with a frown.

"Guy was trying to kill Will," Rachel said quietly. "Not my dad. And my mom attacked Guy, so he had to defend himself."

Ewan spun on his heel to face Rachel. "You're defending him?" he exclaimed, shocked. "He killed our parents! Left us orphans! How can you defend that—that—*creature*?"

Rachel did stand, facing him and putting her hands on her hips. "You're the one who's telling me that the people of The Story are fixed points, and can't make their own choices! He was a victim of that. I don't deny that what he did was wrong, and how much it churns my stomach, but he's not the one at fault here."

Ewan made an irritated noise in the back of his throat. "It seems we're destined not to agree on that," he said stiffly. "Let's talk about something else ... shall we?"

Still indignant, Rachel couldn't even bring herself to look at him. "Like what?"

Obviously searching for something, Ewan walked back to his seat and sat down heavily. "Like—the intruder. How much do you know about him?"

Although that was the last thing Rachel wanted to discuss, she likewise sat down, still stiff and annoyed. "Not much," she said, instinctively reaching up and touching the bump on her head where he'd struck her. "He came to the island and has been destroying The Story in his path to ... whatever it is that he wants. I believe he's gathering an army to take over."

"Bingo on the last part," Ewan said. "But he's not aiming to destroy The Story. He just wants to take over. And, if you're sick of calling him 'the intruder', then just call him Carson. That's his name."

"So how did he know about The Story?" Rachel asked. "Outsiders shouldn't know about its existence!"

"That's an easy one," Ewan said. "He was a Guardian, written in many years ago. I believe he was Merlin? Anyway, he managed to escape The Story somehow, and apparently became bent on getting revenge on the Guardians by taking over The Story and undoing everything they'd worked so hard to maintain since The Story's creation. Granted, I wouldn't really care if he just freed The Story from their control, but he plans on destroying a lot of heroes to get the villains on his side. Not my idea of a good leader."

"How do you know about all of this?" Rachel questioned, her eyebrows shooting up.

Ewan chuckled, though it seemed slightly forced. "He came and offered me a job."

"Oh my gosh, Ewan, he wanted you to *help* him?" Rachel exclaimed, her eyes widening. "Are you serious?"

"Perfectly," Ewan responded. "He thought I was just some random disgraced Guardian that hated being Morpheus. Which, granted, I'm not too thrilled about it, especially lately, but—"

Rachel interrupted him. "Why only lately?" she said.

The question made Ewan shift uncomfortably. Judging from the way he avoided her gaze and stared at the floor, she knew it was something especially bad. "W-well ... it's just ..."

Rachel's eyebrows shot up. She'd never been able to successfully make her brother speechless before. When he saw the look she was giving him, he reddened further. However, in addition to his obvious embarrassment, Rachel could clearly see grief hidden there. "I lost someone important to me," Ewan said, in a significantly softer voice. He turned away from her, towards the fire that he was cooking their breakfast over. Apparently, he wasn't really looking at it, as he didn't see the black smoke puffing out of the top, from the burning eggs. "Permanently. Someone that wasn't supposed to die."

"I don't understand," Rachel said as softly as he did.

"The Story was changing even before Carson got in here," Ewan replied, finally turning back to her. "Red shouldn't be that old. My ... friend ... shouldn't have died."

Judging from his hesitation at the word "friend", Rachel gathered that it was probably a young woman. She didn't press him. It was obvious that the mental wound was still fresh, and she didn't want to hurt him. She never did; sometimes hurtful things just slipped out, and she always wished that she could take them back. "Then what's happening to The Story?" she said finally, hoping to move past the awkward conversation. "Why was it changing before this Carson guy even got here?"

Ewan shook his head helplessly. "I actually don't know. I wish I did, but I don't." He cast about the room, his eyes settling on the door to the outer room. "Rach, there's something I need to tell you."

"You mean, beyond what you've already told me about me traveling with the two people who had the most to do with my parents' death, and that this Carson was the most powerful sorcerer ever and is now gathering an army to destroy The Story?" Rachel said.

Even though Rachel was being serious, he still cracked a smile. "Yes. Beyond that," he answered, and his smile faded slightly. "It's about Will."

"What about Will?" she asked defensively.

"No need to get snippy with me, I'm not going to criticize the kid," Ewan retorted, holding up his hands innocently. "You need to know, though. Our mom and dad died for him. Think about it for a minute. They're sent to save him from getting killed, and the first thing Dad does is hurl himself in front of Gisborne's sword? And then our mom attacks Gisborne, to give Scarlet time to escape. They're doing this for someone they don't even know."

"You said Mom attacked Guy because he killed Dad," Rachel argued, her voice going hoarse as she thought about their parents.

"There was that, but she yelled at him to escape," Ewan said. "*After* her husband died. And I don't know why."

Rachel stared at the floor. "What are you trying to say?" she demanded. "Why did they want Will to escape so badly, if they didn't know him? And how do you know all this, anyway?"

"The—the Guardians told me," Ewan said, stammering slightly. "Anyway, there was something I didn't know about Will until he got here. He's immune to magic. Not only did he survive the Lethe with his memories intact, but I couldn't even look into his mind with my Morpheus powers. You need to keep your eye on him. There's something weird about it."

Although Rachel's mind was running a mile a minute, she made no response. After waiting for a reply that didn't come, Ewan seemed to smell the acrid scent of burning eggs for the first time, and he looked back with a wrinkled nose. "Well, darn. Looks like breakfast's going to be a little late," he said, and tossed the eggs into the fire.

Rachel left her brother mumbling over his cooking and went back into the room with her friends. They were all awake now, and Will had come back in. His legs were splayed out on the floor in front of him as he looked over Red's shoulder. The young woman was reading the Merry Men book and trying not to laugh at Will's constant surprise at the pictures.

Guy was still on his bed, but he was sitting down, his hands folded in front of him. When Rachel came out of the kitchen, he looked at her quizzically. After a moment's hesitation, Rachel jerked her head at the door out to the temple, indicating for him to follow her. Without any hesitation, the knight stood up and followed her out of the temple, to the steps outside.

When Rachel sat down heavily at the top of the stairs, Guy sat down beside her. "Are you well?" he asked after a moment or two or silence. "You look ill."

"Well enough," Rachel mumbled, not meeting his eyes. "I've been talking to Ewan." Thinking about that, she knew it was probably obvious, but she couldn't think of any other way to start the conversation.

"So I noticed," Guy answered in his usual calm manner. "I assume you know now what I've done?"

Rachel glanced at him. His face was entirely serious. "How do you know?"

"You wouldn't have called me out here if it wasn't to do with ... that," Guy answered, his devastating logic defeating Rachel.

"Alright, yes, you're right," she admitted. "I know you murdered my parents."

His serious brown eyes were still intent on her face. "Would you like me to tell you how it came about?" he asked.

Although she'd already heard of it from her brother, she nodded, and Guy nodded back. "Very well. The Merry Men had departed with Robin Hood to the competition with the golden arrow. For some reason, Scarlet wasn't with the rest of them, and my men had spotted him in the forest. When I went after him, I managed to corner him. I believe he'd injured his leg or his ankle. I had him at the point of my sword, and I will confess, I was angry. I was prepared to finish

201

him at that moment, when, from nowhere, a man appeared. I didn't even know who he was, but he just threw himself in front of Scarlet, and I stabbed him instead. As he died, a woman started attacking me. I demanded to know who they were. I didn't want to kill a woman, but she wasn't giving me any choice. She screamed at Scarlet to run. I kept demanding to know who she was and what she'd come for, and she finally answered me. She told me that her name was Miriam Andric, and that I was a dead man."

Rachel bit down on her lip as hard as she could to keep herself from crying. Hearing about her parents' final moments from the man who had killed them was even harder than hearing it from Ewan. "I had no choice, Rachel," Guy said softly. "I aimed to wound her, and spare her life, but at the last moment, she moved. She was trying to stab me and made a fatal mistake. I stabbed her instead." The young man had his eyes squeezed shut. "This was a few Story cycles ago, I suppose. When I met you, and when I'd remembered The Story, I knew. You have your mother's face, and your father's pride, though I knew him only for a brief moment. I came with you because I felt I had to make it up to you, though there is no way that I could."

Rachel gave a choked sob and looked away from him. "Why didn't you tell me sooner?"

"How could I?" Guy demanded, his voice a little shaky. "What could I do? Walk up to you and say, 'By the way, I killed your parents'? You don't understand the effect you have on me, Rachel. There's just something about you that makes me want to ... to impress you. And I knew that wouldn't."

Rachel looked at him through red eyes. "I—I don't know what to do," she said quietly. "I want to be angry, but at the same time, both your story and Ewan's tells me that you didn't intend to kill them. But you did want to murder Will, which … I don't know. I just don't."

Guy stared down at the stairs. "I can return to Nottingham, if you wish."

Rachel stood up, and he did as well, towering over her. "You're not going back to Nottingham," she said decisively. "I need all the help I can get on this quest. But just … just for now … give me some space. Okay?"

"As you wish," Guy replied quietly.

For one mad moment, Rachel wanted to reach up and touch his arm, tell him that she wasn't angry with him. But since she didn't know how she really did feel, she just walked up one step and went back into the temple.

She hoped that he hadn't seen the tears streaming down her cheeks as she left him outside.

Chapter 24: Parting Ways

Ewan's second attempt at scrambled eggs went significantly better than his first. The group sat down to eat them, even Guy, who had come back from outside the temple. Rachel stared down at the table, trying not to meet Guy or Ewan's eyes as she sorted through her complicated emotions. Although Red seemed to latch on to the tension in the room and become even more reticent than normal, Will apparently decided to fill the silence with his own chatter.

As he prattled on about something or other, Rachel found herself watching him. Ewan's story had given vein to some odd thoughts in her mind. Why had her parents died for him? Yes, Rachel liked him; but her parents hadn't known him, not at all. It couldn't have been just for the sake of maintaining The Story—Guardians apparently never risked their lives for people of The Story. If the person underwent Final Death, they would just be replaced. It certainly wasn't worth dying for, or leaving one's young children orphans over.

After several minutes, Will became aware of the fact that Rachel was watching him. He looked up and met her eyes, his face going as red as his surname. All chatter from him halted immediately, and he stared down at his plate, eating his eggs in silence. Most likely, he believed that she was staring at him because he was breaking the silence and it annoyed her. He couldn't be further from the truth, and she sighed silently.

It felt like ages, but breakfast was finally finished, and the group adjourned to the room with all the beds in it. Rachel perched on the edge of one of the beds, and Will was sprawled on the floor. Red sat with her legs crossed over each other, idly turning her club around in her hands. Guy leaned back on his own bed, and Ewan stood in the midst of them.

However, the silence apparently became too much for Red, who said in an ill-tempered manner, "*Bon dieu*, will we just get a move on with this planning part? I have no patience with it!"

Ewan's lips twitched in an amused smile. "Very well, Red," he said, inclining his head towards her. "I've been informed by you and Will that you plan on heading for The Heart of The Story, right? Do any of you know how to get there?"

"Of course not," Rachel said with a hint of impatience. "If we did, we'd already be there, wouldn't we be?"

Ewan held up his hands in a calming gesture. "No need to get snippy, Rach," he told her. "The fact remains, *I* don't know how to get there, either. But I can possibly direct you to someone who does."

"That's not particularly helpful," Guy said mildly.

Judging from the scowl on Ewan's face, he didn't appreciate Guy's interjection. "Helpful or not, I can send you to someone quite knowledgeable and trustworthy, but beyond that, I can't do anything else."

"You keep saying 'you'," Red noticed. "Are you not coming?"

Ewan stared down at the floor. "I, ah, I can't," he mumbled, glancing once at Guy. "I have to try and convince the gods to side with you, Rach. They'll be great assets to your cause, but it'll be a nightmare convincing them."

"Is that your excuse?" Rachel snapped off, horrified. "You're leaving me *again*? You know that whether I fail or succeed, I will never see you again! The least you can do is come with me and be with me until—until the end!" She stood up, clenching her fists by her sides.

"Is that what you want of me?" Ewan demanded. "To have to stand there and let you be with me, yet knowing that to succeed will mean that I'll die? You might get it in your head to not follow through with your plan to restart The Story. The longer I'm with you, the more temptation there will be for you to fail. And I can't let you do that."

The others were looking away uncomfortably, and Rachel would normally have cared. But at that moment, realizing that this might be the final time she'd see her brother, she didn't care. "Must you leave me behind like this?" she asked, her voice shaking. It was one of the first times she'd let her emotions out of her own free will. "Don't you see how much this is killing me? I can't leave you behind!"

"Do you think *I* want to leave *you*?" Ewan retorted. "But it has to be this way, and there will be no more on the subject!"

Rachel remained standing, stiff, but she didn't protest. Once he'd made up his mind, she had no chance of changing it. Red spoke again. "What happens at this *Coeur*?" she questioned.

Shifting from foot to foot, Ewan ran a hand through his hair. "It's where the Guardians go to write people out or in to The Story, and make harder revisions that Guardians can't solve by just going out into a Story."

Guy leaned his head back, watching Ewan. "Speaking of that, why have the Guardians not written the intruder out of The Story? Shouldn't they be the ones dealing with this?"

The question seemed to stump Ewan. "I don't really know," he admitted. "They seem to have gone MIA, to be honest. But until they step up and deal with this, I'm afraid it's mainly Rachel's problem."

Will raised his hand like a naughty schoolboy. "And we plan on writing out the intruder?" he said. "Is that really possible? Can any Guardian just waltz into this Heart place and rewrite everything?"

Again, Ewan seemed stumped. "I don't really know. That's a question for Merlin—the guy I'm going to send you to. Hopefully, it is possible, otherwise, you're just going to have to go for the good old fashioned plan of killing him."

"Why don't we just do that?" Guy muttered. "It would save us a good deal of time."

"Because he's a powerful sorcerer and it will be practically impossible!" Ewan burst out impatiently. "It might save time, yeah—the time it will take him to turn you into a little bug and squish you with his foot!"

"*Je nes comprend pas*," Red interrupted, glaring slightly at anyone who looked at her.

"Um, what?" Will asked.

"What don't you understand?" Ewan said, huffing slightly. He hastily adopted an apologetic look when Red glared at him again.

"*Pardon*. I do not understand why this man seeks to reek such havoc amongst The Story," Red said, growing less irritable. "What does he hope to gain?"

"My guess is he wants to be king of The Story," Guy proposed. "Am I correct?"

"That, and I have reason to believe the intruder, Carson, hates our family," Ewan said, indicating himself and Rachel. Rachel idly wondered if it physically hurt her brother to agree with Guy. "The Andrics seemed to have something to do with him escaping The Story. I don't really know how. I've just been doing a lot of digging since he came and spoke to me a few days ago."

"He spoke to you?" Red asked, her eyebrows shooting up.

"Yes. He came to see me and believed that I would help him. Didn't do his research, apparently. He wants Rachel—alive, for some reason," Ewan added, looking uncomfortable.

Rachel sat down heavily again. "So, for some reason," she said, purposely parroting her brother's words, "he wants to kidnap me? That sounds great."

"Well, don't stress out about that right now," Ewan said. "What you need to worry about is getting to Camelot and getting to Merlin. It won't be easy; I don't know how you'll get an audience with him. He's supposed to be a former Guardian, but if he hasn't recalled The Story, then you're in trouble."

"So we just have to hope that he has," Will said, trying to be optimistic. "Should be easy enough, right? When should we go?"

"Immediately," Rachel replied. "There's no use in waiting." And no use in drawing out her goodbye to her brother, painful as she knew it would be. It would be better to get it over with … wouldn't it? She didn't know, and she didn't want to think about it. Maybe if she just ignored it, the pain would go away.

Ewan's face twitched as he looked at her. "Good point," was all he said. "I can supply each of you with a sword, if you want …?"

"I only need my club," Red told him flatly.

"I'll take a bow and arrows, if you've got it," Will added. "And a sword. I do like to use a sword as well."

Guy shrugged. "A sword will do me well enough."

Rachel nodded in agreement with Guy, and Ewan returned the movement. He left the room and came back a few minutes later, laden with weapons. He dumped them on the floor, the only indication that he was emotional. "All yours," he said shortly, turning away quickly.

Red stared down at the floor, and Rachel saw what resembled a blush rise to her cheeks. "This is foolishness," she said quietly. "We could use all the assistance we can get. And you do not give your sister enough credit."

"Maybe I don't give myself enough credit," Ewan said, his lips twisting bitterly. "Maybe I'm afraid that I'm going to try and convince her not to rewrite The Story, to give myself more time with her. Or maybe ..." He looked at Red, and his face grew more pained. "I'm afraid of getting too attached to people."

Red's eyes widened, and she hastily looked away. Rachel pretended not to notice. After an awkward silence, Will sprang up from his sprawled-out position and scooped up a sword, his bow, and a quiver of arrows. "Well, I suppose we'd better get a move on, right?"

"Right," Rachel said, but it was with heaviness in her voice. It was the very moment that she'd been dreading, and she found herself staring down at the floor. She wished that she was anywhere but there.

Ewan waved his hand at the other three, and belatedly, they left them alone. Rachel noticed with a tiny spark of amusement that both Red and Guy had to drag the unfortunate Will along behind them, out into the temple beyond. Her amusement vanished as she turned her gaze back to Ewan, swallowing past a lump in her throat.

Once they were alone, Ewan took a step towards Rachel, almost hesitant. "Rach, I just—I don't—"

Rachel bit down on her lip. "Ewan, is this it?" she asked, her voice shaking. "Is this the last time we see each other?"

Immediately, her brother enfolded her in an embrace. The feeling of his chin on the crown of her head was oddly comforting. "Don't think like that, sis," he whispered, his voice hoarse. "You know that even if this is the last time, my faith and yours will enable us to meet again someday. It's in God's hands."

Bitter tears slid down Rachel's cheeks, burning her eyes as they fell. "Don't talk like that. Please don't. What comfort is it to me, if you get to be in Heaven while I'm still here?"

"Because it's the comfort that you'll see me again," Ewan affirmed, crouching so the siblings were at eyelevel. "That death is not the end."

"But what if people who undergo Final Death don't go to Heaven?" Rachel asked, sniffing.

Ewan smiled bitterly. "I guess you'll find out eventually," he said. "But we have souls. You and I both know that I was a normal human, just like everyone else. Getting written in didn't change that. So I refuse to believe that Final Death means no Heaven."

"I hope you're right."

"Have faith, Rach," Ewan said, patting her shoulder. "It will go far."

Rachel nodded, trying to stifle her tears. "I'll try, Ewan."

"That's all I can ask." Ewan straightened up again. "Just promise me something. Don't treat Will any differently now than you did before. He deserves better than to be blamed for our mom and dad's death. Just keep your eye on him, and cherish him. Because through him, our parents live on. Okay?"

Rachel glanced over her shoulder, able to distinguish the sound of Will's voice, carrying from the temple outside. It brought a small smile to her face. "Okay," she agreed, turning back to Ewan. "It's a deal."

"And about Guy …" Ewan hesitated. "I don't like him. But it's obvious that you do. And I guess that for once, I need to trust your judgment. So, just be careful around him, and remember that he's a villain. Whether he seems to change or not, he's still got those tendencies. Even if he wants to change, it's going to take time."

"So you're saying I shouldn't trust him?" Rachel said doubtfully.

"I'm saying to tread carefully around him," Ewan replied. "Not that you shouldn't trust him. Because Red is right. I hate to say it, but you're going to need all the help you can get."

Rachel nodded. "Okay. I think I get it." She gave him another hug, trying to ingrain the moment in her memory before she lost him forever. He squeezed back gently, his cheek on the top of her head, and he stroked her hair. "I'm going to miss you, big brother."

"Not as much as I'll miss you," Ewan answered quietly. "But I know you're going to do some great stuff, Rach. So don't think you won't."

"I'd rather do some not-great stuff and still have you," Rachel said, pulling away. She rubbed her eyes. "But I guess that's not my choice now."

"It would seem not," Ewan agreed. "Stay safe, Rachel. Hopefully next time I see you, it'll be in Heaven."

"Not too soon, I hope," Rachel said, forcing a smile. "I'm in no hurry to die. But it's good to know you'll be waiting for me."

"I can appreciate that," Ewan answered. He rubbed his nose in a business-like manner and quickly turned away, clearing his throat. "We may as well call the others in and send you on your way."

Chapter 25: The King's Sorcerer

The massive doors to the throne room of Camelot swung open. Contrary to the doors' immense size, a small figure in black robes walked in, running his hand through his messy jet-black hair as he went. As the doors slammed shut behind him, he approached the lone figure on the throne, rolling up the sleeves of his robes and revealing his thin arms.

Once the young man—little more than a boy—stood in front of the man on the throne, he bowed. "Good day, my lord," he said, raising his deep black eyes to the King. His formal tone and serious eyes contrasted his seemingly-youthful and unmarked face. "Do we have any developments?"

King Arthur sighed, his big hand stroking his blond beard. Although he was hardly out of his mid-twenties, his hair was already becoming ash-colored with grey. Arthur's deep-set grey eyes were wrinkled and sad, aging him years. "I'm afraid not, Merlin."

Merlin Emrys, the King's sorcerer, ducked his head. It grieved him to see the man he'd served for years, looking so old and sad. Very recent events had taken their toll on them both. However, he didn't comment on that, knowing that it would just distress Arthur further. "We'll find something eventually, Arthur," he said quietly. "You can count on that."

"I hope you're right." Arthur leaned back. In both age and physical appearance, he dwarfed Merlin, though the teenage body was simply Merlin's choice. "Have you received any word on the rest of The Story?"

"None yet," Merlin said. "Word hasn't traveled far enough, I suppose. Well, at least we know who's committed this heinous crime …"

"Yes, but there's nothing we can do about it!" Arthur exclaimed, pounding his fist against the arm of his throne. "Without proper evidence, if I accuse Mordred, the people will turn against me. As far as they know, he's still my loyal knight, with his own estate as well."

"I'll think of something," Merlin assured him. "Don't worry. Lancelot and Gawain will be avenged."

The incident the two men were discussing had happened a few days before—almost a week. In the middle of the night, while two of Camelot's finest knights, Lancelot and Gawain, had been patrolling, an unknown assassin had broken in and murdered them both in cold blood. Gawain had died first—shot by an arrow to the back. Lancelot had been unable to defend himself, as he was killed only seconds later.

What made it even worse for Merlin was the fact that he'd come upon them only moments after they had been killed. He'd been with Lancelot as the knight had drawn his last breath. If he'd been only one minute sooner, he might have been able to save them both. It was bad enough that Camelot's two best fighters had been eliminated in such a callous manner. Even worse was the fact that both Arthur and Merlin had been close friends with them, and their loss was personally devastating.

Arthur in particular was taking it hard. "Why would he do this to them?" he asked heavily. "We were always kind to him, and he repays that kindness by murdering them ... his brothers-in-arms. It is true evil and cruelty."

"I did try to warn you," Merlin said softly. "Didn't I say not to give him that estate? Not to honor and spoil him as terribly as you did?"

"Don't rebuke me, Merlin, please," Arthur pleaded. "Don't you think I feel bad enough about it as it is? I don't need you piling more guilt on me!"

It was evident to Merlin that his King was in one of his emotional "moods". The chances of having a logical and calm conversation were slim to none. Yet another day when nothing was going to get done. Fighting down frustration, Merlin inclined his head. "Very well, Your Highness," he said, albeit rather stiffly. "Forgive me."

Before either of them could say anything else, the big doors opened once more, and a very-nervous page walked in. He scrambled over to them and hastily bowed to the King. Once the man got closer, Merlin could see the thin sheen of sweat on his face. "M-my Lord, forgive me," he stammered. "But I thought you should know. She—she's *here*."

The two young men exchanged anxious glances. "*Now*?" Arthur complained. "She's the last thing I need!"

If Merlin was being perfectly honest, the visitor was the last thing he needed as well—perhaps for slightly different reasons than Arthur. Considering his King's current state of mind, Merlin wished that the woman had waited for any other day than this one to come. Then again, if she was coming, it meant she had something to say. And perhaps ... "Maybe we can discern something useful from her," he suggested. "Whether she intends to or not, she might reveal something about the murders, something we can go off of."

Arthur's only response was to cover his face with his hands and give a low, pained groan. Since he didn't answer one way or another, Merlin chose to take it as a positive reply and turned to the page, taking charge. That was the only thing one could do when Arthur was behaving as he was. Sometimes, he acted like the teenager that Merlin had found on the streets and made King. "Send her in," he told the page in a low voice.

The boy bowed in answer and hurried off, panting slightly. Once the boy was gone, Merlin turned to Arthur with a hint of impatience. "You'd best get yourself organized," he said briskly. "She'll be here very soon." Honestly, sometimes it felt as if Merlin had to run Camelot alone, and he wasn't even King!

Arthur gave him a slight glare before adjusting his position on the throne, propping himself up. He straightened his posture, though he was still sending glares in Merlin's direction. Merlin looked down at the floor, trying to conceal his own annoyance. Arthur was a wonderful King—the best Camelot had ever seen—but even the best had their flaws. Arthur tended to let his emotions get in the way of his judgment, which made him more problems than they solved.

As Arthur tried to rearrange his features into one of calm and dignity, the doors swung open once more. Sometimes, Merlin wondered why they didn't just leave them opened. However, his thoughts were quickly distracted by the tall, dignified, raven-haired woman who walked through the doors, her scarlet dress gliding around her feminine and attractive figure. The woman's dark green eyes blinked from under long, luxurious lashes, her chiseled pale face looking as if it were made of glass.

Her heels made clicking sounds on the marble floor as she approached Merlin and Arthur, hair swinging around her waist. She halted and inclined her head, somehow making the gesture insolent. When she raised her beautiful face to them, her green eyes sparkled with humor. "It's always a pleasure to see you, brother," she said in her deep, throaty voice. "You're looking as ... *disheveled* as always."

"Morgana." Merlin was mildly impressed that Arthur managed to not twist his half-sister Morgana le Fay's name into a growl as he normally did. Perhaps he would show more self-restraint than he normally did when speaking to her. "What the devil do you—" Catching the meaningful look

216

Merlin was giving him, Arthur hastily amended his words. "What can I do for you?"

Morgana giggled. "So courteous," she commented. "Is Merlin finally rubbing off on you?" Arthur's face turned red, and he looked away, coughing as he bit back a retort. Morgana laughed again. "It would seem not. So, how are you, my least favorite brother?"

"Morgana, I'm your *only* brother, and a half-brother at that," Arthur snapped at her.

"Not well, then," Morgana said, as if to herself. She started walking forward again.

Merlin put up his hand in warning. "That's quite far enough, Lady Morgana," he said, pitching his voice a little lower than normal. Sometimes, assuming the form of a teenage boy had its detriments. Even with his young appearance, she still knew he was the biggest threat to her in the room.

She stopped, though she adopted a pouty look. "Oh, come now, Merlin. Don't you start getting hostile on me!" she complained. "I only came to *warn* my dear brother. Would you really want to stop me from doing that?"

Merlin was unmoved. "You can warn him just as easily from there." Any charms that woman could possibly have used on him at any time had died along with Uther Pendragon.

Morgana's pout increased. "You're so mean, Merlin," she said. "Well, I suppose I'll have to look past your rudeness. You know the assassin who killed Lancelot and Gawain? He's coming for you, dear brother. You'd better watch yourself."

"And you're telling me this—*why*?" Arthur burst out, unable to control himself. "What have you ever done for me, other than try and steal my throne? You attacked my wife, tried to kill my knights ... mind-controlled my sorcerer!"

Merlin grimaced at the mention of the last incident that Morgana had brought about. He wished Arthur hadn't brought it up, as it certainly hadn't been one of Merlin's finest moments.

Morgana shrugged, even the small movement made graceful. However, her expression grew more serious and less teasing. "I won't pretend to like either of you," she admitted. "However, my reasoning for warning you is more selfish than it is for you. If you should die, our humble Story dies as well. Much as it pains me to say, I've gotten in over my head, and now I have to make certain I don't perish as well."

Although Merlin kept his expression neutral, his mind was rushing about madly. Of course Morgana wouldn't want The Story to be destroyed ... self-preservation had always been foremost in her mind. And if she was admitting to being in "over her head", then she really must have gotten involved in a bad deal, one that she couldn't think of any way out of.

That alone made Merlin believe that she had come honestly, and he softened, just marginally. "And how do we know that we can trust anything you say?"

"You don't," was Morgana's indifferent answer. "If you choose not to, though, I can promise you that by tonight, King Arthur will be dead, and our Story will be collapsing in on itself. Camelot and all its inhabitants will be destroyed, and the only ones to be blamed would be the two thick-headed fools who didn't listen to a friendly warning." With that, she turned gracefully and swept out of the room, her silk gown swishing dramatically around her.

Once she had gone, Arthur's proud look swiftly went with her, and his shoulders slumped. Those sad eyes sought Merlin's face, and he bowed his head slightly. "They're coming to kill me," he said softly.

"With that attitude, they will succeed," Merlin replied. "Rest easy, my lord. Tell the knights to be on their guard, in case the killer tries to come early. In any case, I'll think of something, don't you worry. Camelot will not die tonight."

Arthur sighed. "I hope you're right," he said at last.

"I am." Hopefully.

With that, Merlin bowed respectfully to his King and backed out of the throne room. He had a lot of thinking to do.

.   .   .   .   .

The unthinkable had happened to Rachel. When she stepped through the Story door, she found herself alone. There was no sign of Red, Guy, or Will anywhere. That alone would have made her anxious, but the massive, white-stoned city that she now stood outside of made her even more so. She didn't like crowds, and never had. Such a city as was before her was bound to have people—possibly thousands—thronging the streets.

Still, she had little choice but to enter the city if she was to find the others. After all, Red didn't exactly blend in to the crowd, with her vibrant red cloak. Even Will's height would be an asset. The only problem was that she'd have to go in there, alone, and get shoved about by the mob, babbling and too noisy for her to even think.

Rachel drew in a deep breath and started walking. She wouldn't get anywhere if she didn't start moving. Striding along, she tried to look more confident than she actually felt. She didn't know if she pulled it off. Confidence wasn't exactly her strong suit, though she tried to pretend that it was. In the end, she just had to take a breath and hope for the best.

To Rachel's immense relief, if not confusion, there was no crowd. The streets were entirely devoid of people, and as quiet as the grave. The few people that did wander the streets gave Rachel a wide berth, eyeing her breeches and blouse. The one or two women walking wore billowing skirts, and Rachel didn't match them at all. All she could do was burrow deeper into her cloak and hope nobody looked too closely at her.

From the safety of her cowl, Rachel viewed the streets, trying to find some sign of her friends. But in the widely-spread and solemn figures wandering the streets, there was no sign of any of them. She sighed miserably. After five years alone on an island, the last thing she wanted was to be by herself again.

With her eyes staring down at the street, she heard someone approaching from behind. Just as she raised her head and turned to see who it was, the burly blond man grabbed her from behind. He pulled her close, pinning her arms to her sides, and covered her mouth with his hand. Much as she tried to reach down and draw her sword, the man obviously knew what he was doing in keeping her immobile.

Frustrated both with her inability to do anything and the entire situation, Rachel screamed into his hand, the sound muffled. Even someone standing next to them wouldn't have heard. She struggled and fought, kicking at his shins with her boots.

"Here! What do you think you're doing?" Rachel's captor—and, as a result, Rachel herself—turned to face the impetuous voice addressing them. To Rachel's surprise, the speaker was a boy, in his mid-teens, with mussed raven hair and piercing black eyes. He was barely more than five feet tall, and incredibly thin.

"This is none of your business," the man snapped, holding Rachel closer to him. She struggled, her clear-blue eyes widening in fear. She didn't want to know what her captor intended to do to her, and panic was racing through her. Where were her friends? Why had they left her? Why was she alone?

The boy cocked his head, his gaze locked on Rachel's. "Ahh," he said. "I see." What he saw, Rachel didn't know. And now she couldn't even see him, as her captor was dragging her off, turning her around. Much as she tried to dig her heels, her small size was again a detriment to her, and she could hardly even reach the cobblestones with her heels.

The man grunted in pain. "Let the maiden go," the boy demanded, and the man swung around again. His grip on Rachel's mouth loosened slightly, just enough for her to invent a plan. A disgusting one, but a plan nonetheless.

She bit down on his palm as hard as she could, gagging on the foul taste. The man yelled out and shoved Rachel away, sending her sprawling to the cobblestones. A flash of heat swooped over her head, and the man's yell dissolved into a scream. A strange scent assailed her nostrils—burning flesh. Her former captor scrambled away, and she raised her eyes to the boy who'd saved her. His hand was still smoking from the fireball he'd thrown. "Hello," he said.

Rubbing at her mouth and trying to rid herself of the foul taste on her tongue, she didn't answer. The boy came over and helped her to her feet, thankfully without his hand being on fire. "Judging by your eyes, I'd say you're an Andric," he said. "It's an honor to meet you."

Rachel stared at him, and as a result, saw movement behind him. "Look out!" she yelled, drawing her sword. The boy dove out of the way—well, more tripped, given his ridiculously long and large robes—as a sword hissed through the air where he'd been standing. Two men immediately moved in to take advantage of it, and Rachel stepped forward, praying that the years of training alone on her island would be of service to her now.

Steel clanged on steel as one of the men attacked her. It felt as if Rachel could see all around her, in a perfect circle. She saw the boy getting to his feet, saw the second man advancing on him. The first man was powerful, forcing Rachel's sword to her throat as he held her in a lock. A lock that she couldn't break. The sword got closer, only an inch from her neck ...

Work instinctively. Rely on your gut. It knows what to do best. Ewan's words from so many years ago rang in Rachel's ear. Instinct. Gut-instinct. Her foot shot up, slamming into the man and sending him staggering back. Without waiting for him to recover, she closed the distance between them with a single step. The steel of her blade caught the sunlight as she stabbed forward, detached. Her tunnel-vision blocked out all but the path of her sword, going forward, aiming for the man.

The sword met with resistance. Blinded by desperation and the memory of training with Ewan, Rachel kept going. There was a metallic scent in the air, and a heavy weight on the end of her sword. She jerked on it, and the blade came free. Clarity returned to her as she watched the man sag to the ground, blood covering his torso, his eyes open and unseeing.

I killed him. I killed a man. The sword clattered onto the cobblestones from Rachel's numb fingers. *He's dead.*

"Watch out!" The boy's voice brought her back from the brink, and she ducked, the sword narrowly missing her hair. A zapping noise soared through the air, and the second attacker went flying against a nearby building; he slammed into it and slid to the ground. Rachel stared at him, in a trance. Her gaze slid down to her hands, still clean. The bloodied sword lay on the ground at her feet.

A hand on her shoulder made her jump and swing around, but it was only the boy from earlier. "Well done!" he said. "You inherited Philip's talent, it would seem."

"What's going on?" Rachel demanded, finding her voice. The trembling in her tone made her anxious. "Who are you? Who were those men?"

The teenager largely ignored her, and knelt beside the man she had killed. The man whose last breath she had stolen. Her odd little rescuer didn't seem so much interested in the fact that the man was dead, but more in the black surcoat he was wearing. "Of course," the boy murmured, standing upright and turning back to face her. "It doesn't surprise me that Mordred sent men to kill me. Granted, I wasn't expecting to find a young woman being attacked."

"Mordred," Rachel said, forcing her mind into line. "This is Camelot, then?"

"It is," he replied. "My home. I am called Merlin Emrys by both. It's a pleasure to meet you, Lady Andric."

"You—you're Merlin?" Rachel said, staring at him. She'd always pictured Merlin as a wizened, bearded old man, not a boy barely in the midst of his teens. "But that's—"

The boy, Merlin, smiled in a way that indicated he'd come to expect that reaction. "The truth," he finished for her. "This is my preferred form, though I can look much older if I want to."

"Why?"

"Why would I want to look older? Well, the King's council wouldn't take me very seriously if I didn't," Merlin answered, then seemed to realize he'd misunderstood her question. "Oh, you mean, why do I prefer looking young? Well, you know, it's how I was written in."

"You were written in?" Rachel said, feeling as if he'd left her far behind. "Ewan told me; you're a Guardian."

223

Merlin nodded. "Former Guardian. Written in quite a long time ago. I believe, when your parents were young."

That gave Rachel a pause, staring at him in bemusement. Merlin had known her parents when they were children? "But you look so young ..."

"Because I want to," Merlin said. "Are you even listening to me?"

Rachel frowned at the tone he was using with her. "I'm not an idiot. Excuse me for being a little shell-shocked at what's happened to me." She pointed at the corpse. "I just killed a man!"

"I'd hardly call him a man," Merlin said idly. "He was a killer, cold and cruel. You've probably saved numerous lives by ending his life."

Rachel's hands shook as she looked down at the man's body. "But I killed him. I took his life and now he's never going to breathe again, and it's all my fault."

The young sorcerer stepped towards her and grabbed her arms. "Your name," he said. "What's your name, milady?"

She looked at him, her lips trembling. "It's Rachel," she said. "Rachel Andric."

Merlin smiled at her, guiding her down to the wall and sitting her down. "Rachel Andric. It's a pretty name," he said. "Very pretty. And tell me, Rachel Andric, as the child of two Guardians, there must be a reason you're here, in Camelot. Please enlighten me."

Rachel looked up at him from her seated position. She needed to bring her mind to focus, to slow her racing heart. She had killed, yes. But she was going to have to do it again in the future. "I've come for your help. I need to know about The Heart of The Story."

Merlin looked at her carefully for a few moments, before smiling, his black eyes still obviously scanning Rachel. "Then you've come to the right place, milady," he replied. He extended his hand to Rachel. "Shall we go have a drink and talk about this?"

Rachel hesitated before reaching out and taking his hand. He helped her to her feet. "For The Story," he said, and the two set off together.

Rachel didn't know where her friends were. She didn't know what the future would hold for her. And she didn't know if she was going to be able to figure out what was going on in time to save The Story.

But at least now she wasn't alone.

To be continued ...

Made in the USA
Middletown, DE
14 May 2022